You Are The Boy

by Danny Unrau

Copyright © 2012 by Danny Unrau
First Edition – October 2012

ISBN
978-1-77097-532-3 (Hardcover)
978-1-77097-533-0 (Paperback)
978-1-77097-534-7 (eBook)

Published by:

FriesenPress

Suite 300 – 852 Fort Street
Victoria, BC, Canada V8W 1H8

www.friesenpress.com

Distributed to the trade by The Ingram Book Company

For my family: past, present & future.

Enormous thanks to Lois, for unending support, and Shoshanna, Andrew, Aila, Dean, & Levi for their encouragement, (and specifically Shoshanna for the cover art) and all those who have so kindly encouraged my story-telling.

It should be noted that while some of the characters in this book will seem to some readers to be recognizable, every one of them is a creative conglomeration of persons the author has met, known and invented. Places and dates and events may be geographically and historically accurate, but the story is fictional.

Chapter 1
Cherry Creek, Canada – 1950

She was tired, so tired. She had often thought these last nine months that four children were surely enough, two boys, two girls, a good number and balance, and now six years since the last, another one. And she was so tired. So ill. Too weak for this. The hardest work a woman, any person, can do. Birthing. And now another one. How would she feed it? How would she manage this all? Would the other children help? Would they resent this child? Would her body survive? Would her husband become even more silent? Just do more and more things without speaking, without asking?

They should never have had this one. But what does one do?

Dr. Vogel entered the room. His hand reached for her wrist. "Won't be long, Mam!" he quipped, smiling, reassuring and professional.

Her body convulsed, the waves came, covered the head, took the body. She was too weary to scream, too weak to care. They came and came like waves on a shore, never ending. Pounding waves. How could a human body of flesh and blood, sweat and tears, worry and wondering withstand such overwhelming waves on a weak woman's body giving birth against even her own wishes? Like the waves that grind down rock this was a power within her, within the larger being of a woman that even she could not understand. It stood alone. It took over and it ran as it willed.

The green room, the pewter bowls, the shiny instruments came in and out of view as shadowy nurses and the doctor worked around her, helping, poking, pushing, shouting, calming, reassuring, and finally something relaxed, and then there was a release and a new silence.

A new noise had just entered the world. A boy. Wet, confused, out of sorts, disoriented, no sense of self, no inherent sense of peace, just light that was too bright and air that was too cold, that his senses told him, and he protested, showed the world his immense displeasure. Displeasure, or at least a good deal of cynicism, would that be his standard off and on throughout his life? He would often find a way of enthusiastically letting his world know what he felt. Some would think it was rebellion at his core, others just a simple propensity to mischief, others again just a game he played for fun. Whatever the reason, when he was in the room it would be known, this much would be true.

Outside the birthing room and down the grey corridor, the immigrant husband wrung his worn cap, fingerprints of grease on its peak. Pacing he piously cursed himself at the wisdom, at the stupidity of them having another child. He was worried. Mother, as he always called her now, might not make it. He knew that she was not strong, that she was sick too often. So often he paid little attention. He remembered now how ashen her face had been, how much fright was in her eyes when she had wakened him and said, "It's time!" It was true he did not understand her much of the time, but he still cared. Could she tell? Both his misunderstanding and his caring?

"You've got a son, Mrs. Ruhe. Looks like a healthy boy. A little skinny, but a boy all the way," the dark eyed, dark haired doctor said as he patted her hand.

He turned to leave the room and the cleaning-up to the nurses and aides. She smiled, just a hint. Closed her eyes, then opened them wide, trying to sit up. "Doctor! Doctor! Please, no knife! No cutting! No cutting on the boy! Yes?"

She thought she saw him nod. She closed her eyes again. Escaped. Collapsed. Slept. He was out the door and heading down the hallway of the country hospital. The nervous father heard the doctor coming toward him in the hallway and he stepped forward to address him.

"You've got another boy, Mr. Ruhe," laughed the doctor as he came within arms reach of the farmer father. "Another boy to help you in the fields. With the cows. And the pigs. Another boy on your side against all the women in your house."

"Uh, Dr. Vogel. Good. Thank you! Thank you! My wife, she is in health? Yes?" His words exploded in a staccato that suggested timidity in the presence of this greatly educated and exotic, highly esteemed doctor. His head was full of so many questions but quickly he thought that any questions he could think of would only be a waste of time for this important doctor to answer. "Praise be!" he hurried on, "But I say one word, Doctor? No, what you say, ah, ah, circumceesion! We don't believe in cutting the boys. We have a tradition from the old country. It is always done, you will say, we know, but mother and me, we don't want it. No sign of cutting, okay? We don't cut our boys; our people don't cut. Not anymore!"

Dr. Vogel smiled and shook his head. "Don't worry, Mr. Ruhe. There'll be no cutting. There'll be no circumcision, if that's what you're concerned about and if that's what you want. You can go in and see your wife now, and see the little farmer in the nursery window."

Cap still in nervous hand Jacob moved toward the birthing room, not quite knowing what his most necessary persona at that moment would be, husband or father. Already from the doorway he could see that the exhausted birth-er, Ruthie, had slipped into a deep sleep, her black hair, unkempt, stringy, oily looking, splayed itself across the white pillow around her head as she lay, face up, lips slightly apart, and he was relieved. They would not celebrate this new birth together this day; there would be time and energy for that tomorrow.

The next morning Jacob was at the hospital early and the parents of the new baby visited, and celebrated the gift of this new child. Ruthie had gotten some real rest over night; Jacob had decided it was wise to take the time after he had finished milking the cows to drive the old pickup truck back into town against all the urges to be at work in the fields and in his dilapidated barn with the livestock. She was sitting up in her bed, pillows behind her shoulders, hair brushed, looking rested, more ready to live her life than she thought possible the day before. He sat down in a chair, pulled it up close to the side of her bed. His work boots had been cleaned. His old-country cap, the kind that only new immigrants wore, he twisted and folded and then clamped between his knees as he leaned over and toward his wife. After a quick kiss they prayed together, his farm calloused hand covering hers on the bed covers. He prayed first and then she did, both of them thanking God for the safe arrival of another child, a son, for their other children, their extended family, their heritage and tradition of faith, the church, their daily bread, and protection, especially in this birth. In the practiced habit set by their parents and the people of the sheltered community they had grown up in that they heard praying so often, and in true gratitude they gave thanks for the freedom of this sometimes seemingly still new land. They both ended their respective prayers with the request that they be equipped to somehow be witnesses in this community among a people they could not understand so well even yet.

After their quiet "Amen!" said in unison, they spoke to one another with intensity, straight into one another's eyes as they seamlessly mixed two languages, sometimes three, to make a point, trying to be understood as to what each of them was saying and feeling. Even in this sanctified moment of new parents celebrating a new child they had to work to be in alike world at the same time. Man and woman are not the same in so many ways. But there was in this moment, despite any worries and many differences, a palpable happiness in this birth for both of them. New life always suggests new hope. Ongoing and unwavering hope had served them better than reality in what was now the second decade of their immigrant experience in Canada, and in all this, the birth of another child gave them one more moment of connectedness, hope was continuing.

A nurse coming in to check the postpartum mother stopped at the door, and hearing the couple's murmured conversation wondered whether the two were speaking German, or maybe Yiddish, but noted mostly the intensity in their demeanour, their conversation, both leaning in toward the other. It seemed almost sacred, too electric in its energy, to be disturbed. She moved away from the door and down the hallway on to other tasks. She could come back to this one.

"We'll name him Bobby, just Bobby. Okay?" Ruthie was saying, a statement that faded into a question. "It's such a good Canada name. Everyone will know he will be from here. He won't be so different," she added. She watched her husband; she saw him pull away. Jacob was silent. She already knew that he never said much if he disagreed. Mostly he just went ahead and did what he wanted to do without saying he was going to. He hardly ever argued with her and while those who did not know him very well might have thought he did not hold to many of his opinions very deeply, she knew differently. He never fought. Just kept quiet; stayed silent. He had long ago decided that silence was his best weapon in living with this excitable, passionate woman.

In his later years he would seemingly talk all the time. Driving in their succession of Ford cars, LTD's, preferably Crown Tops, whether alone with Ruthie or relegated to the back seat of his own car holidaying with their grown children on long journeys across the prairies, or through the towns and villages of a number of countries visited in their retirement, he would read the signs on the roadside, or on the business fronts out loud, if no one was speaking. Words in his later years were for filling spaces of silence; in the years of his youth and young adulthood many would have wished he would have spoken up more often. But now, for those same many, it was too much.

The energy of their conversation had subsided, and Ruthie needed to sleep. Jacob stood up. He kissed his wife gently on the forehead, patted her hand, slid the metal chair to the wall as if it were his duty to tidy up, and pulling his cap back onto his head, strode to the hospital exit.

Back in the truck he shifted carefully through the gears and turned north onto the main road that ran through Cherry Creek, south to north. He had to use the gears to control the old pickup's speed, the brakes were hardly working anymore, rounded the second corner he came to and rolled up onto the gravel parking space in front of the Land Titles Office, the only government building in town. Naturally, therefore, the Land Titles Office was where all the births in the region were registered. Jacob Ruhe shuffled into the front office and looked shyly around. The office was in appearance like a bank, with wooden desks and chairs and gently corrugated smoked glass barriers crowning waist high wooden partitions in the same light oak as the rest of the furniture in the office. The receptionist, with a quick smile, asked the fidgety gentleman standing with his cap in his hand and obviously waiting for someone to give him directions, what she could do for him.

"I have come to register the birthing of my new son," he announced, too loudly, he thought, as he spoke. He was always nervous in government buildings, and with English people, for that matter; his memory of corrupt Russian government officials, even though now so long ago, meant he still did not let himself completely trust any kind of officialdom, unless it was of the church, and only then the church he knew. Governments and people other than their own kind had never been deemed to be trustworthy. Hundreds of years of training in that kind of thinking flowed through his blood. "Remain quiet in the land and be separate from all those others," had been the watchwords of his Mennonite people since their time in Prussia before Catherine the Great had invited them to Russia, and even before, all the way back to the 1500s when the Friesian priest, Menno Simons, started his particular protestant movement, and out of which, deliberately or not, came this deeply religious, fiercely private, socially skittish people.

"A son! Well congratulations, Mr, Mr?" the friendly receptionist turned clerk said, smiling and looking for a name, sincerely wanting to relax this man so obviously ill at ease in this office and in her presence.

"Ruhe. My name is Ruhe. Jake is what people here call me. I was called Jakey when I was a little boy in the old country, but my name is Jacob Ruhe." Now even more embarrassed and even more self-conscious suddenly realizing how much he had revealed about himself to this official woman, he hurried on, "Are there papers to write and moneys to pay when there is a birth?"

"Yes, of course, Mr. Ruhe, but don't worry. It's not difficult and it's not much, and I will help you. You tell me what I need to know and I will fill out the forms for you. When and where was your son born?" she asked as she pulled some papers out of the top drawer of the counter between them

"And your son's name?" she asked, already printing something deftly with a fountain pen, both in a long ledger book with blue and red lines, and again on the top page of some loose pages.

"Your new son's name?" she repeated.

Mr. Ruhe was quiet, didn't answer. The clerk paused, noticing his hesitation, and lifted her eyes to look at him, pen poised.

"You have named him already, haven't you?" she asked, something in his manner making her cautious.

"Yes, his mother and me talked. His name is, is, ah, Ben. Yes, yes, we are calling him, Ben." If the woman noticed some uncertainty in the father proclaiming his new son's name, she never let on.

"Does he have a second name, Mr. Ruhe?"

"Ah, no! No. We don't have second names." Then "Yes! Yes! There should be a second name." Too loudly again, he noticed. "Maybe Jacob. His name should be, ah, Ben, Ben Jacob. He is my son. A son of mine. Ben means 'son of.' Yes, his second name should be Jacob. My wife won't mind if I have given him a second name without speaking to her, checking with her." Actually he was concerned about his wife minding at this moment, but he shook himself imperceptibly and looked to the government woman to keep going.

The friendly clerk finished the markings in the ledger book, asked him to add his signature at the bottom, curious, at first, whether he could write, and with a flourish of her pen on the top page of the sheaf of official pages with the edges of tracing paper sticking out between the top two or three, completed her work. She slid the ledger under the counter and lifted up one of the loose pages, setting the others aside into a wire basket on her desk and gave it to him to sign as well, which he did with the same deliberate great care he had signed the ledger. Jacob thanked her and tried not to appear to hurry too quickly out of the room and get safely back to his truck with the official paper in hand. He was confused somehow from his experience of registering his son's birth. The young woman had seemed to be someone who could be trusted, but his wife's expected response to what he had just done maybe was not so soothing to his spirit. Steering his red Ford pickup back to the hospital through the quiet streets, he met no other vehicles. He entered the hospital and walked as deftly as his heavy work boots would allow him down the hallway of the town's only medical facility, stopped at the doorway to his wife's room and peered around the door frame. Her eyes were closed. He was relieved. He tip-toed into the nearly silent room, the only sound being the hum of a fan turning slowly on the ceiling, disturbing lazy, summer flies, and he placed the folded government form, with the name Ben instead of Bobby somewhere on its page, onto the grey metal dresser beside the other things there: a German Bible, Luther's translation, and a wilting carnation in a jar. He had also remembered to bring the crayoned picture that Leina, the only one of his children that had been awake when he was ready to leave the farm earlier in the morning, had drawn and sent along with her Dad "to give to Mom." He slipped out of the room, unnoticed. Back in the truck he turned toward the farm, its black soil, his cows, a tractor needing some repair, the older children who would all be awake now, and would have been given their breakfast by their oldest sister, possibly some neighbours who needed a mechanical favour, his private thoughts and his safe silence.

Chapter 2
Slavgorod/Barnaul Colony, Siberia – 1922

The village was really a collective of farms, long narrow strips of land bunched along the winding road as it snaked across the Siberian *steppe*. Houses and barns clung together like husband and wife, or maybe more like two drunks, a row of them on each side of the road, dusty in summer, muddy in spring, frozen hard in winter. Each narrow property touching the road claimed some additional land to itself beyond the village limits and shared, too, some community pasture land for the livestock. Village boys, usually the ones considered too slow to do school work, or too uninterested in book things to be anything but a nuisance to the requisite stern teacher and those who wanted to learn, took turns herding and guarding the cattle for the whole community from late spring to the first threat of snowflakes in fall.

Life was still rather simple and relatively uncomplicated here in Siberia. The Revolution had begun in 1917 and Tsar Nicholas II had been assassinated a year later, to be sure, but all that seemed yet to be happening only in Petersburg and Moscow, and seemed so far away. For so long unscrupulous priests and leaders of the Russian Orthodox church, the mostly unruly armies of whatever colour they declared themselves to be and any others of one privilege or another had worked to make life easier for themselves, all of which had almost always made life harder for the peasants and those who were not part of the court, the military, or the civil service, but at this great distance from the centre the turmoil was often blessedly distilled.

The village, Schönwiese, or 'beautiful field', like its neighbouring villages, was a Mennonite one, in a reserve or colony of many of them. While the term Mennonite might be best understood to be describing a people, the Mennonites were a religious sect that saw itself evolving from an ethnicity into a kind of nationality, but spared the curse of believing there was a land reserved for them somewhere by God and biblical evidence. Everything these folk touched or owned, and even ate, took on the hue of their identity, so it was not inaccurate to say that their villages were Mennonite. At least as Mennonite as their own adaptations of *borscht, leba wurst, rebspair,* church music, tight community morés, and a certain *dhimi* demeanour as required when with people of a different ethnicity and faith. Schönwiese, and the villages surrounding it for some *versts,* had become home to a group of Mennonites here in southern Siberia since they had moved east from the Molotschna, Arkadak, Neu Samara, and other settlements in west Russia that this people had established after they had been invited by Catherine the Great, more than a hundred years earlier to take up Russian residence and citizenship.

These Mennonites, or Anabaptists, as they were sometimes known, when described theologically, were followers of the ideas of Menno Simons, though they attached no real reverence to him nor made any kind of saint out of the Friesian priest of the early to mid 1500s. His leadership and influence stemmed from his having turned significantly away from his Catholic roots by dangerously baptizing consenting adults when they asked for the rite in spite of their having been already baptized as infants by their parish priests at the request of their parents. This new religious community marked by this new baptism followed somewhat, though only somewhat, in the thinking of Martin Luther and any number of other reformers of the age. The Mennonites would come to suffer terribly for their treasonous religious and political rebellion against the power and control of the Catholic Church, and its supporting princes, and those who had not been flung into rivers or burned at fiery stakes had scurried or silently drifted to the safer regions of Europe, with many ending up in Prussia. There they made names for themselves in various unique ways, some positive, some negative, and were once again harassed and persecuted by the authorities for their beliefs before they were offered a kind of liberation and a chance to begin anew through access to rich agricultural Russian land and opportunity, free choice in religion, faith practice, education, and a clear promise of no military duty for their sons, ever, in the lap of Mother Russia.

So the Mennonites picked up their belongings and established themselves in the Ukraine beginning in Chortitza in the 1780s and the Molotschna in the early 1800s, and moved on to Arkadak and Neu-Samara further east thereafter. When these places, too, became overburdened with too many people for the land holdings they had acquired, crop failures and other disasters, particular groupings headed east to Siberia in the early 1900s. Over time they built their villages: small houses, barns, large estates, schools, mills, dairies, blacksmith shops, farm equipment sales and repair centres, and, of course, churches, just as they had in their earlier settlements.

There had not been much contact with outsiders such as *Die Russa*, (the Russians) nor anyone else non-Mennonite, and that lack of contact was thought good, though they were quite open to some fraternity with the exotic and nomadic *Khirgiz* with their camels and heavy coats, even in summer, who came into their villages from time to time looking for food, old metal containers, especially those made of copper, tubs, horses, and even horse hair previously trimmed from

DANNY UNRAU

horse manes and tails and saved by the Mennonite farmers for a time such as this. Travelling bands of Gypsies, too, would set up their encampments on the edge of the Mennonite villages. They would try to draw crowds with their medicines and singing and dancing, though they could never get much more than blank stares and some simple condescending giggles from the more forward children who ventured cautiously and without community and parental permission out to the Gypsy fires and colourfully decorated wagons. The Russians who came into the Mennonite villages, and had to be dealt with for economic and other trade reasons, were tolerated, and the Jews who had risked leaving the *Pale of Settlement,* and had also relocated in Siberia, well, the Jews, if they could ignore the frank spiritual and cultural attacks of the usually passively aggressive Mennonites on their own turf, were welcome to work as tailors and other kinds of domestic service providers and traders, as long as they understood that only certain homes were open to them, and that they had better move on when their required work was done.

Every few years or so one of the Mennonite sons, and less often, one of the Mennonite daughters ran off with the travelling ethnic bands who were in the neighbourhood or were passing through, but mostly the community held its own. Really, held its own.

Franz Ruhe pulled the sheet down over the window, as the children, ten of them (typhus had not yet made its deadly visit) scrambled for their prescribed places at the long rough wooden table before Mother was motioned to light the candles before dinner. She pulled a satin ribbon across her forehead, placed a white cloth on her head, lit the candles used only on this occasion and said: *May God bless you and protect you. May God's face shine toward you and show you favor. May God look favorably upon you and grant you peace.* It had to be

Friday night; this little ritual took place only on Friday nights and only in the Ruhe home.

Jakey, they called him, though Jacob was his registered name, was twelve. He was the eldest and at this stage of his life, a talker. "Papa," he asked, "why do we do this, with these candles? Why is this night different from all the others? And besides," he complained, "no one else in the village does this, with the mother praying. Other Mennonite women don't pray, except right after their husbands in church, aloud. In other homes the candles are just lit when it becomes dark, and a woman never prays, except when the men are cutting wood, or in the fields, or away in Slavgorod or Novosibirsk? Why do we do this, Father?" Jakey's voice was edged and ringing with the sound of more complaining and criticism than wondering; there was more embarrassment stirring in his rebellious nature at his family's peculiar ways than really wanting to know why they were doing what they did on Friday nights. What was significant for him was the potential criticism he knew his family was open to receiving in the village were this Friday night practice to become known; he sensed there was something Jewish about this praying ritual, and doing something Jewish would not be welcomed in this staunchly Mennonite community, nor anywhere in openly anti-Semitic Russia. This he already knew.

"Mother prays because I will it," answered his father, Franz, sternly, not a man given too much to explaining his actions to anyone, let alone a boy not yet thirteen. Father's tone ended the audible questioning, even though the boy wanted to ask a larger question of their differentness in this Mennonite village, but it remained unasked. He was beginning to learn silence.

"Eat your soup, Jakey," coached his mother, having set her prayer utensils of ribbon and head cloth aside, as she set a large wooden bowl of steaming food in the centre of the table, reachable to all hands. "I'll need your help with the baby soon."

Father Franz scowled with what looked like a touch of worry, his eyes meeting his wife's briefly. She knew what he was thinking, but would not let on. In the meantime, the children helped themselves to generous slices of black bread spread with lard and vied for quick access to the soup which had been ladled from the enormous cooking pot hung over the fire into the large bowl that now stood at the centre of the table. Their spoons reaching in and out of the bowl from every angle around the table and clashing with one another almost like swords in battle could not contain all the precious bits of meat, pork it was, in the melee of the children's take and grab. Being siblings there was more at stake than just empty bellies in their competitive frenzy for food.

"Herr Singer, the tailor, comes tomorrow," announced Franz between slurps of soup seemingly strained through his thick mustache, carrot bits caught in his beard, causing humour to dance in the children's eyes, their energy mysteriously raised by the fearsome prospect of Papa seeing them laughing at him. Such would never be tolerated, hence the humorous danger. Sometimes danger is funny, or maybe some things are made funny by potential danger.

"And this year Jakey gets a suit for his birthday, his thirteenth birthday, and I think, don't you, too, Mother, that you and the girls should get something this time?" Franz pronounced more than asked.

Mother smiled, but protested a little, knowing her politics. "Maybe it should be you too, Papa, who gets a new coat for going to town to do business. And for leading the choir. If you should become choir conductor?" But Franz had made his decision, as was his duty.

Jakey would get his suit and the girls some new blouses to try on once the tailor, Herr Singer, had set up his sewing machine, named Singer, too, interestingly enough, which he had brought with him last year for the first time, and had so proudly shown off to Mother along with his selection of cloth for the year. Herr Singer would sew their things the first day, and after spending the night in the barn loft, comfortable on a thick layer of hay, others of the village would come the second and third day to be measured for clothes from this Jewish tailor who only stayed at Franz Ruhe's house, who only sewed there. The neighbours sometimes talked about why 'the Jew' would only eat and sleep and work at the Ruhe home, but really they did not mind, they would rather he did not stay with them anyway. Most, in fact, would not allow it even if pressed. Jews were not welcome in their Christian homes. It was sometimes whispered around their meetings with Russians that the Jews were the ones who had killed Christ, and that they met in secret groups to plan to take over the world. Always prudent Mennonites would know it would not be wise to fraternize too closely with Jews. One never knew what might be important in the future.

The Ruhe children liked the tailor. After the meals while still sitting at the table he told many stories. Stories both hilarious and stories very sad. Stories of great teachers in small villages, *shtetls,* he had taught them, with greater lessons, and stories of miracles. His stories almost seemed like they could have come from the Bible, though the children had never heard these stories in church. And when the tailor was there, the food was different, somehow. Even better, the boys could wear their caps in the house, even at meals, at the table. They thought maybe Papa allowed such so that the tailor would not feel so all alone with his little hat that they thought he did not take off even to sleep. And yet, the children knew it was a rare day in this village when anyone but a Mennonite was made to feel anything but uncomfortable. That was one way non-violent people could overpower, or at least intimidate others.

The social technique of causing others discomfort the older children of the community had intuitively begun to understand and employ.

Herr Singer, the Jewish tailor arrived early the next morning. The two men greeted one another warmly with enthusiastic shouts, great bear hugs and back slaps, and the exchange of kisses. The tailor worked all day as was his custom: measuring, cutting and sewing. The meals were as they always were when he was their guest. In the evening after they were sent to bed, the children could hear the muffled voices of their father and the tailor talking, and arguing, of course, about their common Bible, at least part of it, and their two respective faiths, their similarities and their differences. These conversations were mostly about their two peoples, both seeing themselves as chosen, the Mennonites believing they were called to dispense a quiet salvation, the Jews thinking they were called to dispense righteousness to their world. The two men easily agreed that to be called by God was much more a responsibility than a privilege, and in the end, often felt more like a hardship than a blessing. Nevertheless, in spite of feeling remarkably safe with one another, the Mennonite villager and the travelling Jewish tailor raised their voices to emphasize their own positions. Franz stating that humans are by nature since Adam "fallen" and that the increasing violence around them was a result of that sin gone wild, and Singer, on the other hand, wanting to be clear that he did not believe in the Fall, that Adam and Eve's failings were no theological issue for his people. It was the Jewish people's repeated and ongoing unfaithfulness to God and their unwillingness to live out *HaShem's* commandments that was causing their oppression through the violence being visited upon them as a people almost everywhere in the world, he would say. The discussions between these two men were spirited and passionate, yet deeply respectful.

"You are a remarkable man for a Christian," Isaak Singer commented one day near the end of one of their many discussions.

"Why would you say that? It is not good for a man to hear that he is considered remarkable. It goes to pride," countered Franz Ruhe, "but I am curious at your statement, especially, 'for a Christian' as if you don't expect much." Franz's question was not as innocent as it might have sounded.

"Oh, we expect much," laughed Isaak, "but most of it not good. In fact we do not expect much kindness or acceptance from Christians. We have lived too long; and not long enough, too often. The good neighbourliness I have received from you is an exception to our entire history. But how do you know all this about Jews?"

"I came to know much about the Jews and their beliefs, and their practices," answered Franz, "from a good Jewish friend when I was young back in the Ukraine. I was many times in his home in one of their settlements at the end of our village fields. My friend had said his father was something of a *Rebbe*, or a *melamed*, I think he called him, I don't remember exactly. I saw how your people love the Bible, the Torah, I saw how they even kiss the book before they read and pray, and I heard how they pray every day to love the One Lord their God with all their might. I was also often with them at the beginning of *Shabbas*, and some of their *Shabbas* worship practices my wife and I have instituted into our family so that we stay close to God, so that our children remember. I have not gone so far as to put a *mezuzah* on my doorpost to touch, nor have I asked my boys to tie prayers onto their forearms for strength, and foreheads for thinking, though I admit the Bible prescribes it, and I should obey. I have spiritualized some Jewish material practices, as I think you people have done now that there is no Temple anymore in Jerusalem, but on Friday nights each week at a special dinner we pray like you Jews do. We believe that we worshippers of God should allow ourselves to be reminded of Him at every opportunity, and certain practices and habits help. You Jews understand that well."

"That is why I say you are remarkable, Franz," the tailor continued. "We Jews rarely hear of a Christian who doesn't want to kill us, in reality, or at least through conversion, let alone mimic us in prayer. Who has heard of such a thing?"

"I believe God still has a plan for the Jews," opined Franz. "Our part of the Bible remains clear on that. It is no accident, however tragic, that so much of the world hates Jews, but I think we who want to know God should not risk hating the Chosen Ones. That could make life go bad for us. It is also not in the spirit of our Jesus, *Jeshuah*, who was a Jew, I remind you, to hate. It was he, as a Jew, too, who said we should make disciples of all people lest you want to chide me for proselytizing again. Nevertheless, my point is that he said 'love', he did not say, 'hate and treat badly', he said 'love'. I believe that being kind, and even being friends, when we can, is something found somewhere in the action of love as taught by our Saviour, or as you would say, our Rebbe."

"Are you not afraid that the others may call you a Jew lover and because of that experience some of what we experience?" asked Isaak, choosing to ignore some of the direct and indirect implications of what Franz had just said.

"It is a risk. It is a risk. But I have a confession that may speak to some lack of courage on my and our part as a people. Since the anarchists have been terrorizing both your villages and ours, these past twenty years or so, we Mennonites have stopped circumcising our sons as we once did. Sometimes the brigands are making the boys show themselves when they come to our villages to terrorize, and the circumcised ones are called out of the line-ups and are asked where they live. They are called Jew-boys, and have been treated badly, and worse, if they have no foreskin. So as a people in our villages we have decided to no longer circumcise our sons. Do you think we are cowards?"

"I guess if you want to disassociate from us, I am somewhat sad," Herr Singer replied, "but, then, you are not called to carry what we carry. 'Why would you live by the 613 laws of Moses when the seven of Noah will do the same for you', the rabbis say to the Gentiles when asked, but if you want to save the lives of your children, you can do no other. I have often wondered how far I would go to save my children's lives given the opportunity, given a small choice in the middle of a horror. It is something we talk about in our synagogues on many occasions." Often the lamp burnt low before Isaak Singer, the Jewish tailor, and Franz Ruhe, the Mennonite, would go to their respective beds.

It became clear to the children of this Mennonite home that their father entered into conversations with Herr Singer both because he liked him and because he desired to exercise and increase his own faith. The tailor probably engaged so willingly in these conversations for the same reasons: for the friendship of another person and out of the desire to increase his own understanding. Besides, he must have missed the normally vibrant everyday exchange in his own community where he was so seldom able to be anymore as he wandered far and wide to make a sparse living.

Over the years, and their infrequent visits, the two men had become fraternal brothers, a rare thing for two men of these disparate faiths. An even rarer phenomenon in early twentieth century Russia which did not encourage tolerance and understanding between divergent groups. Fear and the dismissal of differing views, even violently overpowering those who were different, was far more the norm.

Neither of the two men were given much to laughter, but they did laugh together, like they laughed with virtually no one else. The Ruhe children sensed in these two men a unique friendship demonstrated by their comfort in disputation and their distinctively demonstrated affection. What was more, the children sensed, given a kind of rhythm in the men's voices that seeped through the rough wall of the house between the children's sleeping room and the kitchen, where the men sat at the table for their conversations late at night, that they prayed together. As if a Jew and a Mennonite respecting one another was not enough, the thought of them praying together was almost beyond imagining.

Jakey wondered about them praying together as he drifted off to sleep some nights after straining so hard to listen in on their conversations, hoping not to miss a single word these men shared, but by morning he thought he must have just imagined or dreamt the spiritual unthinkable, their father, the Mennonite choir leader and sometimes lay preacher, praying with the tailor, a Jew, and the impression faded. Jakey never asked his father about it; and never with any of his siblings did he talk about his impression that their Papa, the Mennonite, and Herr Singer, the Jew, prayed together. He remembered it only years later far away in another world when a Jewish junkman would come looking for throwaway items on the Canadian farm he owned as an immigrant Mennonite adult learning a new language, but still living the same faith and carrying some of the same affections as his father before him. Some things simply pass down through families unconsciously but concretely. Little could Franz Ruhe and Isaak Singer have known how much their attitudes and behavior of tolerance and affection would affect the destiny of these children in subsequent years and generations.

Chapter 3
Cherry Creek, Canada – 1958

The half dozen boys were behind the barn, sitting on a high wooden plank fence that served as a corral and a holding pen for the cattle. With giggles of excitement and a little repressed sense of horror, they watched the men stoke the fire with wood and coal, push the branding irons further into the centre of the red glow, check the readiness of the huge veterinary syringe, and see to it again that the little vials of animal medicine from the veterinarian's office were at hand. It was branding, de-horning, castrating and inoculating day on the farm. The boys' excitement was due to the inherent violence signalled in the readied tools of the day: branding irons, de-horners, burdizzos and knives, syringes, and bottles of mixed antiseptics and disinfectants to pour into the wounds and apply to the incisions, where appropriate, to the fixed, protected, sometimes temporarily maimed, and sometimes permanently changed animals. All of this understated violence stood against what was normally a much more pastoral place and in the season of spring which mixed the smells of mature and new manure, mauve lilacs, newly sprouting grass, pineapple weed and foxtail in the prairie barnyard. About to be added to these smells was that of singed animal hair and burnt flesh.

As they sat on their shaky perch atop the wooden fence of the rough two by six planks nailed onto home cut mixed oak and poplar fence posts, the boys noticed an old truck, sporting shabby makeshift wooden sides for a box and rusty fenders nearly falling off, come wobbling up the lane, its muffler-less motor roaring. The truck pulled up to the barn and stopped in a cloud of dust, motor wheezing and brakes screeching next to where the boys were anticipating and contemplating what necessary animal husbandry mutilations they would see, subconsciously feeling their own barely emerging manhood somehow threatened by the things about to be done to the male-membered beasts being readied by the farmers-turned-cowboys and the older boys feeling responsible and important and grown-up enough to be included in the volatile, hard and sometimes dangerous work that nearly always required quickness and strength.

"It's the Jew!" shouted Ben. "The junk man." He was not sure if he should use a favourable description to reflect his father's friendly attitude toward the pedlar or a derogatory one to align himself with the fathers of the neighbours' boys sitting beside him on the fence. Somehow his announcement reflected both, and he waited to see which way the fencely mob would react to the junk-dealer before deciding how he would speak of this eccentric and exotic visitation, this other-cultural arrival on the farm. The junkman usually came when none of the neighbours were present, when there was a given friendly family dynamic and not an unpredictable group mentality ruling the day. Ben knew intuitively there could be some uncertainty in the relational dynamics this day between the junkman, his father, well respected and known by most as Mr. R, and the neighbours themselves.

Ben was a boy who already in his pre-teen years could see contradictions in his world and within his own being; a psychologist might have described him as "conflicted." Like his father he did not always know whether he should please himself or please those around him. While boyhood dilemmas of swearing and smoking dried ragweed with one crowd of wild cousins, and being clean-mouthed and Sunday schoolish with another, and the teenage contradictions of drinking beer with one set of teenage friends and being an avowed teetotaler with another, did finally resolve themselves with some sense of a differentiated self and a set of standards that he could more comfortably live with later on in life, this double-mindedness would persist in some subtle ways within Ben well into his middle-age and beyond.

As an eight year old, though, the biggest problem right now was to conciliate himself to whatever his fence partners might think, and still happily greet the junkman whom he loved to listen to and watch whenever he limped his old truck into their farmyard and stayed for hours. The look the junkman presented, the smell he emitted, the stories he told, and the curiosity and the focused intensity with which he rooted through the wrecked stuff in their yard every time he came to their place to find "diamonds" in the junk in so many places, was an adventure to behold.

In the same sort of way the junkman could find gems in junk, Ben grew up wanting to find the gems of the person in the junk of the lives of the people he would encounter when he became an adult and a teacher, a clergyman, a counselor, a world traveler and story-teller. This value he learned from both his father and the junkman.

"My Dad says Jews just want to control the world," said Richard, one of the older boys.

"The Jews killed Jesus," added little Squeaky, only brave enough to add to a conversation if he was sure he would not get punched for it.

"Oh look, the branding irons are red hot!" Ben leapt into the conversation pointing to distract his fence mates' attention. He jumped down to go meet the junkdealer, now stiffly getting out of his old truck. He had never come to the Ruhe farm when there were so many people around; again Ben wondered whether it was wise for the Jew to show up today. The junkman, nevertheless, tousled the boy's hair and said, "Someday I have to tell you the story about why boys should always wear hats," his eyes twinkling with affection. Taking in the situation of Jacob and his neighbours all set to get busy with their animals, and having now suddenly been disturbed by his arrival, he turned from Ben and moved to the fire next to the "squeeze machine," a wooden apparatus with a move-able inner wall into which every animal being treated would be herded one by one in order to be held steady for the proce-dure each individual beast was due.

"Good morn-eeng, Jacob," the junkman shouted through a wide smile at Jacob Ruhe as he simultaneously nodded a greeting to the three or four neighbours and come-lately cowboy wranglers ready to do their day's duty with Jacob's mixed herd of beef cattle, and then later on, the weanling pigs needing to be castrated.

"Want to help, Saul?" Jacob asked, a welcoming grin on his face.

"No, I look for broken theengs, and then go farther, I theenk," Saul, the junkman responded. He seemed uncom-fortable. Perhaps he was sorry he would not get to spend some easy time talking with Jacob this morning. It had been some time since he had visited and his life as an itinerant Jewish junk dealer in this part of the world, while not dangerous, was most likely very lonely. Ben saw him tip his hat, flatten it to one side of his head, and move back toward his truck.

"Check with the wife, Saul, she might have some stuff you can use, or at least a cookie and coffee or something for you to eat. Want to stay for lunch?" Jacob called after him but not losing focus on the job at hand.

"No. No. I go!" the junkman stuttered. He nodded, almost bowed, and hauled himself up onto the broken seat of his truck, a spring and some felt poking up through the worn, torn seat cover. Ben was disappointed he would not be hearing any stories today and he climbed back onto his seat on the fence. His fence-mates were quiet as all of them watched the truck lumber down the lane and turned onto the road, a cloud of white-blue smoke behind it, high-slatted sides wobbling back and forth and some of the junk already loaded in the back from previous stops almost falling out between the slats. Saul, the junkman, had not even looked around as he said he was going to, he had not checked with Ben's mother for whatever she might have for him, including some baking and coffee. Ben was puzzled. He had never seen the junkman so anxious to get going, to leave so soon.

"Why do people hate the Jews, Papa?" Ben asked his father later that night after everyone had gone for the day and Jacob was cleaning up around the barn.

"I'm not sure," Jacob answered, glancing at his son as he reached for a five-gallon feed pail to turn upside down and sit on. "There is no good reason for it, in my thinking! I really don't know. It was the same in Russia. And there your grandfather was kind to the Jews. We had a Jewish tailor who often came to our place when I was a boy, and we loved when he came to our house, and his stories, too, but many people in our village weren't very kind to him. I never understood. But it was not talked about. Not at church; not in the fields or in our homes. People just didn't like the Jews. We didn't even know very many." Ben leaned against a wooden stanchion in the barn close to where his father was sitting on the over-turned five gallon pail and relished his father thinking out loud and the time being taken to talk. As Jacob stood up to get back to work, he added, "I don't know if Mom ever told you that she worked for a Jewish family in Winnipeg when she was eighteen or twenty years old, and before she and I were married. I know there are some furniture and paint and fur businesses in

Winnipeg owned by Jewish people, and some other travelling buyers and sellers, like Saul who comes here. He would never hurt anyone. But you are right, people seem to not like them. How do you know all this?"

"We heard a story in school about the Nazi concentration camps in Germany during World War 11, and the boys sitting on the fence this morning said that the Jews killed Jesus and want to control the world. Is that true, Dad? Does our Bible say Jews killed Jesus? I thought our sins killed Jesus. When Reverend Doerksen preaches, when he starts to cry, takes out his handkerchief and blows his nose like a goose, and then starts to yell as if he is very angry at us, it sounds like he is blaming us for Jesus' dying. There are pictures in our Sunday School books of Jews at Jesus' trial and the Roman soldiers taking Jesus, but now I don't know who killed Jesus. Why are the boys saying that?"

Jacob Ruhe rubbed his son's head. "The Jews didn't kill Jesus, Ben. The Jews didn't kill Jesus. You're right. And your friends on the fence shouldn't say those things. It makes me sad to hear that they're talking that way. We know and like Saul, he is kind and there is no meanness in him. He doesn't have work like anyone we know, so he is unusual, but that doesn't make him bad, does it?" He sighed, and remembered again to resume his work. "Here, Ben, help me get these pigs back in their pen. Let's see if they are recovered enough from their cuttings to want to eat something. After we've got them penned up, you can go to the house and get the slop pail, okay?" Ben moved toward where the pigs had been temporarily held in the corner of the barn, but he remembered his father's hand on his head as much as his words, and even in his eight year old sensibilities he knew that this talk had been important.

Chapter 4
Blumstein/Blyumshteyn, The Ukraine — 1876

A dozen or so *burdei,* half-dugout sod houses with poplar rafters protruding here and there through the uneven sod sections, were sheltered from sight by a thick stand of poplar and oak trees on three sides, and could only be seen from across the Molochnaya River. They should have never been mistaken for being the habitation of even the poorest of humans. These rough shelters appeared to have been squeezed between the ends of the narrow fields of the Mennonite farmers of Blumstein and the bank of the milky waters of the river. As unfit for human habitation as they might have appeared to those who might have seen them, they were the domicile of a group of desperately poor Jewish people, who could not yet refer to their hastily built settlement as a *shtetl* which is what the Jewish villages of the Yiddish speaking world were called. They had gathered in this place and cobbled together sod chunks and thin tree trunks over dugouts to create a village as inconspicuously as they could hoping to never again attract any attention after they had escaped some of the most horrible manifestations of anti-Semitism yet again. To have made such a place home shouted out that these were a people who knew what it was to be under siege. Jews had religiously, politically, socially, culturally, economically, and even militarily, in some manner of speaking, been under siege in many parts of the world for thousands of years for no reason other than the fact that they were Jews. Here in the Ukraine the Russian Tsar's had largely institutionalized anti-Semitism and even made it respectable with the creation of the *Pale of Settlement*, and it was commonly held by most peoples in Russia that the Jews could be blamed for anything and everything: plagues, diseases, bitter water, harsh winters, miscarriages, red spots on the Host at the services of Holy Eucharist, wars, and economic downturns. That these wretchedly poor Jewish folk huddling to the very fingernail edge of existence in the portions of the country to which they were relegated and restricted could be deemed part of an international conspiracy to control the world should have been laughable to everyone, except that this bloody notion had cost the lives of hundreds of thousands of innocent folk everywhere any kind of bigot with a violent streak could find a Jew for centuries already. Like the people of the biblical Nehemiah's re-building the walls of Jerusalem, these farmers and tailors, brewers, milkmen and wood workers, seemed to have to work with *one hand on their swords,* any old discarded firearm they might own, always alert so as not to be struck dead where they were standing. Again, just because they were Jews.

Grigory and Rivka Schwenberg were one of the couples that lived with their three children, all five of them in the one room, in this new settlement that they began to refer to in their Yiddish dialect as Blyumshteyn. Yet two adults and three children in one family was not considered a large family for the times. "G-d has not given me more yet," giggled Rivka to her friends, emphasizing the "yet" although she was almost forty. Grigory, once upon a time a full-time tailor was now sewing clothes only at night by lantern or candlelight for the people of the surrounding villages that were mostly Mennonite or Russian, or infrequently across the river, the Doukhobors, but worked by day, out of severe necessity, on the estate of one of the local landowners, a big and sometimes brutish Russian and Polish speaking man. Alongside his extensive land holdings, this farmer owned sheep and goats, cattle by the dozens and a corral full of pigs. Grigory's fellow workers made sure 'the Jew' got the lion's share of the pig-minding, knowing full well how distasteful it was for him to be around these creatures of complete and utter uncleanness, beasts proscribed by his religion.

It was increasingly difficult for Grigory to fill the mouths of his children and have some food left over to give to the poor who were coming to his door more and more these days, but he was sincerely still able to say, "But G-d, blessed be He, has always provided smiles." So Grigory was open to the possibility of another child, and, like an added Sabbath blessing, the attempts at having one were always a special joy to him as well, for he was a poor man with little entertainment. Rivka simply yearned for another baby, for one more blessing from G-d, for one more signal from *HaShem* that He could still bless them, that "G-d, blessed be He!" would not just leave them to the ravages of their fragile existence. That He was still open to blessing them in their hardships. Rivka's children and her husband's love for her were among the few and best indicators that her life was not completely unblessed, though "Next year in Jerusalem," the prayer-wish that kept the faith of Jews glowing in hard times all around the Diaspora for centuries was beginning to feel more like a wish for eternity these days for her and Grigory. It was no illusion that life was getting harder for these inhabitants here in the *Pale of Settlement* where they were allowed to live, but still relegated to poverty and under so much outside and official control and unmitigated persecution.

The Schwenbergs like their Jewish countrymen everywhere in the Pale had few options but to live under the Tsar's rules having to pay double taxes, forbidden to lease land, run taverns or receive higher education. They huddled in their

DANNY UNRAU

communities and tried somehow to live inconspicuously, and interestingly, close to some Mennonite settlements and villages, and some other non-Russian ethnic groups for trade and protection, hoping, praying, just to be left alone in the midst of a maelstrom of disturbing changes occurring in this so-called great land already dangerous.

Once there were enough families huddled together in Blyumshteyn to make the community spiritually viable in being able to raise at least an occasional *minyan,* the Schwenbergs and their neighbours constructed their very own synagogue that looked more like a *sukkah* than a real *shul,* but it served the purpose of centering their little community and their lives. They had considered deeply and argued vehemently amongst themselves for some time as to the earthly wisdom of building their own synagogue knowing that having it might well cause their existence to become more widely known in the area, but in the end they concluded that faith had never needed to depend on earthly wisdom, and besides it might be a sign from Above that they were not yet abandoned.

In the meantime it came up in conversation between the few Jews and their sometimes friendly Mennonite day employers, that it was the same Tsarina Catherine who had so kindly invited the Mennonites to come live in her land, with other benefits, some one hundred years earlier that had instituted the creation of the Pale of Settlement with its multitudinous restrictions upon the Jews. Some Mennonites lamented the restrictions put on the Jews; others were not so kind. And said so. What they all agreed on was that in creating the Pale, Russian officialdom had at the very least condoned excruciating discriminations against the Jews, and more often than not turned a blind eye to explicit acts of bigotry and violence.

One day, Rivka's Blyumshteyn companions spreading their newly washed clothes on the rocks by the riverside to dry noticed that unmistakable change in her body movements that only women discern ahead of more obvious signs. She herself had suspected for some weeks that she was pregnant. She had wondered about the chances of it happening, given how much her husband had been turning to her these nights of late. Men turn to their wives more at night when things are going badly. She had noticed such tendencies in every difficult period since the very beginning of their marriage. She had remembered, too, that her mother had told her just before her wedding that men seek comfort in their women's arms and charms rather than speak the words that things are not well. Nonetheless her keen feminine intuition had informed her before her body did that at last she was with child again. Opposite emotions of ecstasy and dread flashed through her being. Excitement and foreboding struggled within her. "But that's what it is to be Jewish anyway," she said aloud to herself walking home with a bucket of water, her spirit both brimming and anxious. "It's as though G-d has ordained this strange co-existence of eagerness and trepidation. Maybe that's what it means to be chosen?" she mused. "Why do no other people seem to know that to be chosen means respon-sibility, not privilege? Why do so many people of the world believe it is their duty to reverse and flatten out and expunge what they perceive to be the Jewish privilege of being chosen? It is not a privilege. It is a hard calling. It has cost so much; I fear it will cost yet so much more." Her mind took to ponder-ing the fate of her people alongside the worries for the new life just beginning to swell her body. She pulled up her free hand as she approached the entrance to her hut and laid her arm across her mid-section as if already needing to protect that life

Her body expanded. Rivka told her sister-in-law and the rest of her neighbors that she was pregnant and now all the women of their little community knew that she was expecting.

DANNY UNRAU

It became a welcome distraction for all the women as they went down to the river for water in the mornings. Soon Rivka noticed that she was starting to show earlier than she had with the first three. Before long her sister-in-law wondered out loud over a cup of *kvas* one morning whether Rivka was having twins, even asked whether there had ever been twins in the family before. There had been indeed.

As Rivka's pregnancy progressed, so did trouble in the local Jewish *shtetls* and the Mennonite villages and other ethnic villages as well. Russian bandits more and more rode into the villages on their horses, helped themselves to the livestock, ordered the farmers to stack up sacks of grain for them, and to hand over their tools, especially those that could easily be made into weapons. They took the best horses if they felt some need for a horse, and they took any and all of the rest of the livestock too, some to eat, the rest for target practice. There were rumors of molestation and rape, but no one spoke of those things. Sex, healthy or unhealthy, was considered outside the realm of daily conversation for these earthy villagers, and even outside the exchange between husbands and wives. Conversations about the rapes were never begun.

Seven, then eight months passed. Rivka knew now that there were twins. Food became scarcer and the bandits discovered Blyumshteyn, having seen its cobbled together buildings from across the river. They came around on a regular basis pleased that they had found a community of Jews. Going from hut to hut, the bandits started to demand food at gunpoint from what potato bins, smoked meat reserves and crudely constructed ice-cellars they could find. Prayers in the tiny Sabbath synagogue turned increasingly to requests for protection. The men of Blyumshteyn pondered uncovering any hidden rifles they had and considered oiling and readying them in case they might need them. It was not outside of their imaginings that their small, unprotected Jewish settlement would often be the first place the hooligans would hit as they began their rounds. Guards were stationed in the trees around the three sides of Blyumshteyn. Pogroms were not new and were becoming less uncommon, smaller unreported harassments and local horrors were common. The horrifying past and the present in the experience of the Russian Jew became indistinguishable in this time.

A little bread for breakfast, no midday meal except some shriveled carrots or brown cabbage or wrinkled dried apples from the larder, if they could be found, and hopefully a little something hot for supper became the norm in the Schwenberg home. Rivka knew her swollen belly with her not-yet-born babies was not getting enough sustenance; she began to worry even more of what would happen to these twins after they were born. What would their lives be like? Where would they end up? Would fate keep them together or tear them apart?

Grigory absented himself from a few days of work for the rich landowner who did not always pay him anyway, harnessed himself to his old high-wheeled cart and trudged afield with the hope of some sewing assignments, the offer to transport whatever any farmers and merchants might need moved from one place to another, and tied to the bottom of his cart, were some hand tools he had made to sell to the Mennonite villagers in Blumstein or in any of the villages on the way to Halbstadt. With his tailoring skill he brought his specialty needles, a variety of sewing thread and even some cloth he still had, along with him. He needed work; food he did not worry about, that he would usually get where he found work. He well knew that he could not expect to eat kosher on these journeys from village to village seeking to make a meager living. Added to the prospect of finding food along the way was the knowledge that his being away from home would leave more food for Rivka and the children.

Grigory was hoping, too, that he might have some conversation with the mostly gentle villagers of these German-speaking, somewhat Yiddish understanding, Mennonite communities, about protection, about how to stand up to the travelling outlaws against whom it seemed there was so little protection. Grigory knew that the Mennonites were avowed pacifists, but surely they would not just cave in to these monsters, he thought, as he pulled his wooden wheeled cart from village to village, through rutted hard dirt roads on dry days and muddy, ankle-deep slop on the rainy ones.

There was a reserved kind of mutuality between the Jews and the Mennonites, sometimes, most of the time, in this region of the Ukraine referred to as Molotschna by the Mennonites. Gentleness more often than not overrode the spiritual arrogance of the Mennonites, separatists themselves, still speaking German, deliberately eschewing the Russian as much as they could, even after a hundred years or more away from Prussia and its German language. Despite their gentleness, the Mennonites were sometimes quick to share the "good news" of their Christian gospel with any Jew temporarily in their villages, or in any kind of business relationship and exchange. Nevertheless, Grigory sensed a common love for the Bible and its stories and its God with most of these bearded men, many of whom could easily be mistaken for a Jew at the Thursday markets wherever they were held in the Molotschna, all the way to Chortitza, and anywhere Mennonites had made themselves at home in the arms of mother Russia.

Grigory had little hope left for a good life in Russia. The only thought of warmth he could muster outside the reality of his own people was the experience of a certain kinship with some of the Mennonites in the villages he would visit. He was of the positive mindset that the bad experiences visited upon his people were, for the most part, the antics and the workings of the ignorant. "Not all people are ignorant," Grigory thought. "Praise be!"

He trudged up the slight rise into Blumstein, a smallish but relatively progressive Mennonite village. His shoulders ached from the thick leather bands that hitched him to his wagon, but his heart ached even more, from the awareness of his dire situation and from missing his children and his beloved Rivka. He wondered how his Rivka was doing. He knew he would not sell many of the tools he had made and brought with him. With some of the same trouble in their villages with the travelling bandits, poor crops and a besieged local economy, few Mennonite villagers could afford to buy anything, leave alone hire him for a few hours of sewing. He needed to have something to take back to Rivka; he needed to have faith that G-d would provide. His spirit was prone to worry.

His one happy thought, *schlepping* his wheeled load into Blumstein, was of the quiet welcome he would get from an emerging friendship with David Ratzlaff, for whom he had sewn clothes in the past. Ratzlaff was the esteemed village teacher and a churchman, to be sure, and even the main leader of his church, that Grigory knew. He understood that a church leader must be something akin to being a rabbi, but Ratzlaff was a gentle man who seemed to celebrate the God they shared rather than despaired of the religious differences between them. Grigory also knew the routine in the village of Blumstein. He would be welcome only in David's home. And he would be fed there. Mrs. Ratzlaff would make sure no pork, nor would cheese and meat together on the same plate ever be served, and interestingly — and at this Grigory smiled — David's sons would be allowed to wear their hats in the house, "Out of respect for our guest," David would smile to his sons, though still not at the meal times when he, the Jewish tailor, was there.

Grigory knew that he and Ratzlaff would sit at night after their long days of work, drinking *kvas* and sharing stories mixing their vocabularies of Russian, Low German and Yiddish. Sometimes their talk went "beyond the lines" a little, as they explored one another's faith and life. Ratzlaff was a rather formal man. He was very strict with his children. He demanded that they always dress well when outside their home, not play in the streets and never laugh in public. He insisted that they must uphold their father's reputation as a teacher and minister. So David was stiffer than Grigory in style and deportment, as Grigory with eyes flashing would tease and be playful with children, but the two came to appreciate one another. They both would have said that they looked forward to their infrequent but at least one time a year meetings. Trust of one another more than knowledge of one another was growing between them. Grigory had once told his wife Rivka after trudging home from Blumstein to their own home that if they ever needed help from the Mennonites David Ratzlaff was the person he thought he could go to. "His deep faith in God makes him honourable, I think. As it should," he said.

Chapter 5
Dachau, Germany — 1938

The guard shouted obscenities at the women pushing the waste-wagon up the rise toward the gate of the Dachau Concentration Camp. They were supposed to be hurrying to dump its contents outside the otherwise impenetrable border; they seemed to be taking forever this morning. "*Herr Gott Sacrament!*" he hissed. "*Mach schnell!*" These *sauber frauen* were the rare among the very few people that ever got outside the walls of this hell. Clad in their makeshift footwear hived together from discarded shoes and other bits of cloth and leather and laces left behind by those who were gone, these women had long ago given up any attempts at staving off any "uncleanness." Many of them had lived ritually clean lives in the past as ultra-religious Jewish women through the careful control of what they came in contact with, where they went, and their ritual bathing after menstruation and childbirth, and even relations with their husbands. But now, ever since they had been rounded up and brought to Dachau, such efforts and even thinking about such religious niceties had ceased. Their hauling of human excrement out of the camp and into the woods outside its walls everyday for weeks and, for some of them now, months, had erased nearly every lingering memory of decency in the deep wells of their previously subscribed to spiritual and otherwise "cleanliness" consciousness. But while their deepest religious desires had been put into denial, they still wanted to live; some spark of dignity still remained within their human and feminine spirits. This work was not life in any sense of what the Hebrew greeting "*Chai*" meant, but their daily work did mean that they were still alive.

"Surely *HaShem,* the giver of life, blessed be He, will honour us for our efforts at survival," they thought. "Surely in a place such as this, in a world such as this, in a time such as this, this work is some kind of righteous work," they would quip to one another sometimes to encourage and to retain some semblance of decency and humanness even in the form of some dark humour alive in their existence. They hoped they were right. When hope they still allowed themselves.

The brute shouting obscenities at the woman slopping human shit, was — surprisingly, maybe, but maybe not — Walter Becker, the youngest son of a peaceful, pious, Mennonite farmer-minister in southwestern Germany. Being Schwäbish Walter would greet his fellow Schwäbs in the camp with "*Von wo bischen du her?*" (From where are you?) intoning the unique singsong of the Schwäbish dialect, but once in a while he forgot that the greeting "*Grüss Gott*" was forbidden in this hellhole and he shouted it out to his colleagues. Schwäbs seemed to engender more warmth and charm in their personalities than those from other more formal regions of Germany, but that warmth and charm was not valued in this setting, and as such was hardly ever revealed anywhere in Camp Dachau, and certainly never around the camp's inmates.

While the Becker family Walter grew up in had not in any way lived at the level of the local baron, who spent most of his time hunting or travelling abroad, they did have considerable agricultural landholdings. Their house, though not a castle, was large and reputed to be some three hundred years old and, as most good sized farms, known in the area by its name: the Biegelhof. The walls of the main buildings were close to a metre thick, mortar and rock, and built in a U shape that included an attached chicken barn, machine shed, egg sorting station, other rooms for a range of required utilities and, of course, the family residence.

Walter had been bred, bent, shaped, taught and spiritually nurtured in the strict little Mennonite congregation of Horsbach which met in a small tan stucco, red-tile roofed church building in a farm village up the valley from Biegelhof. Dark clothing and a kind of dourness intended to reflect the seriousness with which the members of the Horsbach Church took their faith dominated the congregational culture. Walter's father was an ordained minister and the main leader of this small congregation, but Walter's rational mindset at this point in his life, more influenced by the public German educational system than the church, left him cool to matters of faith, at least faith as he saw it expressed in his church, though as an idealistic youth he had been somewhat attracted to the Anabaptist teaching of non-resistance and pacifism. In the end, though, Walter had not embraced the peace position of his faith community enough to counter the social pressure that arose as Germany moved toward war in the 1930s, and as Hitler began to show that he might be a leader capable of restoring Germany to its former greatness, to the spiritual reclamation of the great German anthem, *Deutschland, Deutshland Über Alles.*

As the German army was reformed after World War I, motivated in no small way by the mortification of the Treaty of Versailles, a humiliation felt by so many Germans, Walter was caught up in the momentum of building the new and powerful Germany articulated by Hitler and his pure German movement. By the middle of World War II, he had become "a leader in training" assigned to the concentration camp at Dachau, some kilometres from Munich, and not more than two hours from Biegelhof.

As a rising underling in the cruel Nazi camp system, Walter was placed in charge of the *Scheisskommando,* a troupe of female prisoners whose job it was to rid the camp of human excrement. It was Walter's responsibility to see that they did their work of keeping the camp clean without escaping, without making contact with any others coming and going from the camp.

Dachau, its very existence , and the treatment of the people it housed, contravened something within him at first, but he shoved those feelings down and soon he was rationalizing that he was serving his nation, following orders, respecting even the sense of the Bible in the assertion that national leaders are chosen by God, and quietly he did as he was told. Walter had learned under the thumb of his strict father to obey any authority over him. The suggestion that obedience to authority was the stuff of godliness had come easily to the young Walter in his home and his church; and despite the rejection of some things Christian as a young adult he still retained many attitudes and aspect of his childhood faith. It had been so thoroughly bred into the theological bones of every church-going child, especially one so geographically close to Switzerland with its Calvinistic tendencies and collective memory, and was not so easily jettisoned.

When some of the soldiers wondered, first in training and then again in the staff barracks at Dachau, whether with a name like Becker, Walter might be of Jewish ancestry, he was quick to show how strident a follower of Hitler he had become. He passionately denied there was any Jewish blood anywhere in his background and pontificated with his fellow guards how much he hated the Jews, how much they could be blamed for Germany's problems, for the rise of communism and even for the loss of World War I. He added to his credibility and tried to endear himself to his superiors in the sick way of camp protocol by being as inhumane to his charges as he could be. Feelings of compassion that sometimes arose when he let himself see the horror of the prisoners' circumstances, when he dared let himself see the look in their eyes, he pushed away, compensating for what he feared was weakness by being even more horrendous in his treatment of the inmates he was responsible for whenever his commanders were present. This was not the first war in which soldiers had learned to be double-minded; every soldier everywhere in order to be effective in the battle and remain human has had to learn this skill. Walter was no different than most. He too wanted to survive. Most of the people he was in charge of would not be so lucky as to even get a chance to survive if the war went on too long. Dachau by virtue of its reason for being had the stench of terror about it. Any place that people are held in helpless captivity, seen as worthless and treated worse than animals, reeks.

Because Walter was in charge of the *Scheisskommando,* he witnessed the hard work and determination, and even more, the compassion of the women in his detail as daily any one of them would do something extra to cover the weakness of the illness of a sister, or share a precious, final bread crust or cry in sympathy. They reminded him of the women in his life before this war: his mother and grandmother, his aunts, or the women of his childhood church, stepping in when someone was too ill or too broken to continue. Sometimes Walter forgot himself then and saw these "burden bearers" as human beings. But such lapses were dangerous for an up and coming Nazi soldier who wanted to also survive. Always, always, after a slip into slight stirrings of compassion, he made life for the women more miserable with a food restriction, a beating, or some newly invented horror upon one of his victims to reassure himself that he was on the right track. Nevertheless, he sensed that his creeping inconsistency was noticed by his superiors and kept him from moving up the ranks at the

DANNY UNRAU

speed he had hoped for. He was noticed for his loyalty to the cause of a pure-race Germany, but he knew he was not yet trusted sufficiently to ever become an officer in Dachau. Some spark of remembered grace, perhaps in recalling the passing Gypsy who had noticed their barns on fire and had then, surprisingly, helped them save the barns, taking nothing, when he was a child, or something that had printed itself in his soul as he had slumped in the benches of a Mennonite church as a youngster, but still was captured by the story of a good Samaritan, kept him just short of the degradation needed to be a complete hero in the German concentration camp machine no matter how hard he tried.

Day after day Walter marshalled the women who had been chosen and those who had volunteered to be part of the crew that carried the camp's human excrement outside its walls, and oversaw their work. Clearly the women who volunteered for this humiliating and nauseating work did so for the sole reason that it got them past the walls of the camp. The brief foray beyond the walls, albeit tightly controlled, was itself a kind of freedom. It kept alive the dream that maybe, just maybe, their dirty job might someday produce a chance at escape. Beyond its limited rewards of a step outside the wall, and its ever-so-slight hope of escape, the brief encounters with "human shadows" in the woods while dumping the excrement provided these hardy women with the dangerous opportunity of smuggling goods in and out of the camp, and therefore enabled them to make enough extra money to eat just a little more, and to gain some of those things they needed and wanted to share with those whom they loved inside the walls. In the Dachaus of the world, almost anything can be rationalized, not only the horrifying negativity and violence, but even the positive creativity of people wanting to ward off the horrendous and various faces of death, living and real. Daily these women saw something remarkable in one another in some act of kindness toward a sister being overcome or in refusing to inwardly submit to some uniformed beast, in ways both horrifying and magnificent.

Sophia was a relatively old woman, probably too old to effectively be one of the *Scheisskommando* brigade. She told her colleagues that she thought she was somewhere in her mid to late sixties; she could not remember how many birthdays she had celebrated nor her actual birth date. Too many horrors visited upon her as a woman, as a person, had wiped out even good memories, and bare facts. She had a vague recollection of having been in another concentration camp, but more and more that time seemed to belong to someone else. But she was strong for her age, stronger than most of the much younger women in the dirty detail. She could pull a wagon with great determination. That strength and determination made her a leader among the cadre of the women who always smelled badly because of their work, women who bizarrely often dreamed of the French perfumes they once had owned. The odours they exuded aside, these women had some things most of the other women in Dachau did not because of their access to contraband barter. That favour paid off materially and physically, emotionally and spiritually.

Almost everyone who ever encountered Sophia found her unique, even in this place of stressed and diminished personalities. Acquaintances would comment that she conveyed an extraordinary power, the psychological strength and determination of two people. Sophia could be tough; she could also be spectacularly compassionate. She cared deeply for those around her given half a chance and a reason. Her charisma and ability to influence others was remarkable.

Sophia's family had drifted down from the north of Germany into Mannheim in the south sometime after the first War. While they were culturally Jewish, her parents, Grigory and Rivka Schwenberg, had never made much of their heritage as a religion after they had somehow survived pogroms and poverty in the Ukraine, and escaped from Russia some decades earlier to make a new life in Germany. Their children, who had taken up the family's small leather goods making factory, were shocked when suddenly their shop was blacklisted by the "badge" and signage pasted on the front window of their shop by German soldiers, which prevented non-Jews from availing themselves of its services. This was not the free land of opportunity they had thought Germany had promised to be. In spite of their efforts to assimilate, others had known that they were Jews. They felt themselves wrongly persecuted on the one hand, but on the other, found themselves becoming more connected with their sense of peoplehood as Jews. Deep rivers of identity stirred within their family system. Identity is an issue for everyone, whether loudly or silently, it is always an issue.

Sophia knew little of the story of her family's persecution in the Ukraine, beyond that her family had fled while she was a baby. She had survived the pogroms, but as a child so young she had no memory of those events and could not remember any personal horrors. In rare moments, her father, whether from too much ritual wine on Shabbat Friday nights, or because he really wanted the story told, despite its difficulty in telling, talked of life in their tiny village of Blyumshteyn that they had established next to a group of villages made up of people called Mennonites, wistfully of her mother who had died soon after they came to Germany, and sometimes, with great pain, of Sophie's twin sister named Anna who had somehow ended up somewhere else, maybe even being some-body else. Whether he could not remember the whole story anymore, or simply because he could not bring himself to tell all he knew, Sophia never learned more than these fragments. The heavy emotion she saw in her father's face when he spoke of those days, and the natural disinterestedness of youth in things past when she could have asked, had kept her from posing such questions or even wanting to know. Sometimes, awake in her bunk at Dachau tormented by lice, she wondered what might be her story and whether there might still be anyone who knew it. She wondered about that twin, Anna, and that wondering helped her forget the present, and helped her push down the bitterness from suffering for simply being a Jew, something she had never before the war really thought or done too much about.

Chapter 6
Slavgorod, Barnaul Colony, Siberia — 1920

With Slavgorod so far afield from St. Petersburg and Moscow, and even too far from its own nearest major city, Novosibrsk, for the authorities to pay much attention, any scoundrel or group of disorderly, angry, unstable or displaced young men could do enormous damage and immense violence with impunity. One could wonder why it is that civility seems only to slightly propagate itself over long periods of time while bigotry and violence can spread everywhere with seemingly effortless lightning speed. So bands of bandits and desperadoes travelled about the backcountry of Russia and Siberia far away from responsibility to anything and without any accountability to anyone, raping, stealing, pillaging, and doing whatever else their malicious imaginations could run to.

The Mennonite villagers of Russia with their known theological beliefs and practice of peace and nonresistance had always been relatively passive and quite easy to pick on and pick clean, but a certain unpredictability of response was arising in many villages these days as a new generation of more aggressive young leaders were suddenly not so adverse to defending themselves, theology or no theology of peace. Their capacity to absorb so much abuse, so much powerlessness, was running thin; they had had enough.

Next to the Mennonites, the Jews in their respective communities in these outlying areas were, it seemed, even easier to harass, and the crazed outlaws knew that absolutely nothing official would ever be done about whatever atrocities they committed anyway. The roving gangs with criminal leanings that sought out the Jews for their horrific shenanigans piggy backed on a bizarre notion that had traversed the globe unabated for eons, purporting that Jews as a collective had hoards of money stashed away despite the signs of abject poverty in so many of their communities, especially in Russia. Added to that notion was the outrageous belief that whether they were rabbis or tailors, teachers, merchants or solders, all Jews were part of a secret world-wide conspiracy that would keep them away from starvation and always within reach of some power waiting to pounce on and overcome the whole world.

These ideas were gossiped so widely it was only inevitable that by the early twentieth century these incendiary ideas and completely false notions about Jewish people would be published in a contrived and bogus Russian tract called *The Protocols of the Elders of Zion* which would only fan the flames of anti-Semitism higher. This tract of fraudulent ideas would simply feed more irrationality, bigotry, fanaticism and racism and lead to open violence against Jews around the world. In a century that had promised more civility than ever and in what had seemed an increasingly liberal Germany, for instance, it gave rise to the Nazi party and its horrifying policies and practices before the century was two decades deep.

So it was not so surprising that riding a wave of unchecked anti-Semitism and carrying enough anger and outrage to know no limits to their behaviour, a band of miscreants happened upon a small and mostly agricultural settlement of Jews next to a huddle of wealthier looking Mennonite villages, and an estate or two, in Siberia where the Revolution had hardly yet made a dent in the society and the rule of law was largely nonexistent. "We'll be able to pick both, or all three tonight," one of the bandits mused, "Jews, Mennonites and money."

"The hidden money from the Christ-killer Jews, some warm flesh from those soft Mennonite girls whose fathers won't lift a hand to protect them, and some rich food from the fat *kulaks*," laughed Molosovich, a roaming anarchist and a minor warlord of sorts who had an evil glint in his eyes. His henchmen laughed and spit enthusiastically. This was going to be, by their definition, a good night.

As night fell the outlaws half-heartedly doused their fires, took last swigs on what was left at the bottom of their bottles of horrible tasting but crazily potent homemade wine and barley beer taken from Russian villagers the day before, and mounted their horses. They rode to the edge of the Jewish village. One of them started a fire in the long brown grass next to one of the small barns on the edge of the settlement and they watched it eat its way across a little dip in the field before it crept up the log and mud-caked wall. It was probable that the Jewish villagers knew that the dozen or so mounted wild men were hovering in the neighbourhood and were up to no good but no one dared come out to see, nor even to douse the fire that was now hungrily consuming the shed at the edge of their collective. Everyone always hoped and prayed these bands would just move on and keep going, whenever they appeared. As the rowdies watched the flames lick higher up the wall and into the thatched roof of the little barn probably used for sheltering sheep and goats in winter, and of little use the rest of the year, they decided they would come back to this village later if they felt like it. The people of this village were now frightened, they reasoned, and as readied as they could be for what might come later. By now some of the horsemen were feeling other urges. "Let's go see if we can find some gentle and pure Mennonite girls," shouted one of them. "This fire will do its work of warming everyone up here. I'm hot already." The laughter of his evil associates only encouraged the joker's depravation and stoked all of their devious imaginations. They moved in the direction of the Mennonite village.

The village sentries, boys who normally herded the cattle by day, had already noticed the clutch of horsemen and had notified the men of Schönwiese, a smaller Mennonite village amongst many in the Barnaul Colony, that Molosovich and his outlaws were on their way. Some of the parents sent their daughters to the upper levels of their barns with instructions to dig into the hay if they heard the men come into their homes; some of the grandmothers and the older women went to the school which doubled as a church building to pray. Outside the village store a not-so-new argument arose again between the older men and a group of younger ones

"We have some guns for hunting," shouted Peter Reimer, trying not to be disrespectful of these seniors who were ministers in the church, and teachers and, therefore, the leaders of the community. "The Lord would want us to exercise justice, to protect the innocent and the weak," his voice rose. "We should not let these men set our agendas. In defending ourselves we would not be letting them force us to be violent in response to their violence visited upon us. We would be letting the Holy Spirit of our Father God exercise righteousness through us in stopping these men visiting their violent sins against others. We must stand up to them!"

Jasch Loewen, always calm, always one to accept leadership responsibility, responded with a note of condescension in his voice, "No, Peter, we must not bear arms. We are called to love our enemies. Shooting them is hardly love. Love will prevail, Peter, you will see. In time. If we show these men that we will not lift a hand, eventually they will not lift a hand. Grace begets grace as violence begets violence. 'Live by the sword, die by the sword', don't you believe that Peter?" He continued without waiting for the younger man to answer, "Yes, they will eat our food and frighten us with their wildness, at first, but I do not believe that they will hurt any of us. God will protect us. Love always prevails over hate; order always overcomes chaos. It is ordained."

"Not always!" shouted Peter, frustration turning to anger with him. "Look at history! And what of the rumours from our people in the Molotschna and Arkadak? We have heard that barns are being burned, livestock stolen, and the women violated. The times are worsening. You know that, Brother Loewen! And they have done even more damage to the Jews; they have killed people in the Jewish villages. These men see us as weak fools, stupid followers of a weak god."

Peter became aware of the fear of more than just the armed men in his soul. Something was changing within him and it frightened him, but he continued. "They are impervious to our grace, our potential love, which I daresay we have little of, as witnessed how separated from our world we have been for so long. They are brutes, these men, they come only to satisfy their own whims. They don't know what love is. They live to satisfy their own desires and drives. We must save ourselves, brethren, and hope to save them from themselves. God would will that we do so. Surely Christ who cleared the Temple swinging a whip would understand the *Selbstschutz*. Standing up for our brothers and sisters is the same as standing up for God. Being assertive, moving ahead, is the essence of the Great Commandment to love God and love our neighbour, and the truth of the Great Commission to tell, no, to show others that God seeks justice. Then maybe they will see that He is love. Now they are incapable of seeing that. I understand your idea of love, Jasche, but love is sometimes difficult. I have seen you spank your children because you love them, Brother Loewen. Love isn't always soft. Don't you see that's what we need here? Hard love? These bandits are less than a *stadia* away now. We must do something! We must! I beg you!"

The village men looked furtively back in the direction of their own homes as they suddenly felt more vulnerable than ever with this kind of talk. Conflict of any kind had always been difficult for them. Had they as a people been mistaken, thinking that being passive was the same as being non-resistant? Deep down they wanted to have this discussion, just as deeply they did not, but they knew that now, today, there was no time. Perhaps there never would be. They knew that when there were no brigands at the gate, the discussion would not seem to be necessary. The strong believers in passive peace knew what they believed, the lesser believers were ready to talk, and then maybe fight, but no one seemed able to get the conversation meaningfully started let alone resolved.

As the argument unwound at the store, the riders had reached the first house at the western end of the village. Smoke from the Jewish *shtetl* down the road rose into the air behind them. There was a reckless but relaxed nonchalance about the brigand riders, the hidden sentries noticed; later they would wonder if these terrorists might not, at first, have had the energy and the will to do much damage that day if circumstances had been different.

Peter Reimer and Jasch Loewen, Menno Ratzlaff and Victor Mensch, from where they were standing, saw the dozen riders stop in the narrow street in front of the Günther home. It was obvious that they were discussing whether they would go further into the village or not, whether this was a day to sport with the Mennonites or not. Peter wanted to run for his hidden gun. Respect for his elders and their traditional nonresistance stance bolted him to the ground.

Then the Mennonite men saw big Abe Neufeld come out of his house between them and the horsemen, would-be marauders. Abe stood nearly two metres tall and he seemed nearly as broad across his chest. He was a huge, formidable man, and although not usually given to the kind of courage often displayed by men of his stature, on this evening he strode straight toward the armed men, still sitting on their restless horses, with a determined stride and an attitude of strength, but carefully without an air of outward aggression, however. The intruders' horses were snorting, switching their tails, stamping their feet, and rattling their bridles. Abe's dog was beside him as he walked. Neufeld knew that he was placing his life in the hands of these volatile men, that this might be his last walk down his street, his last conversation. But a calm strength drove him that day; he sensed that he was being led and he was a little surprised at how peaceful he felt despite the twist of fear in his belly. His dog stayed close to his master's side sensing his fear, or, perhaps as animals do, knowing that a storm was about to be unleashed.

The men on horseback were at first surprised by the apparent bravado of the man approaching them. Seeing the big man coming up the street, Molosovich's first lieutenant started to reach for his weapon — the riders were armed with rifles or smaller guns — but then he and they all seemed to relax and the horsemen took on looks of bemusement. They could see that this massive man coming toward them, while imposing, was unarmed and projected so little aggressiveness there was nothing to be afraid of. They had had enough experience with the Mennonites to know that only words were used in the fighting they do, and words to these bandits meant almost nothing. Words were cheap. So they waited for this Goliath figure to come near. Interestingly, it was the big man who was picking up the metaphorical and emotional five smooth stones for the ensuing battle out of his prayerful mind and spirit; he really felt like little David going up against Goliath, but not sure he had the equipment he needed. But he was no prophet; he could not anticipate what hell was about to be unleashed before his eyes.

"Good evening, comrades," Neufeld greeted the horse-men, in his German accented Russian, as he drew near them. The mounted men were by this time very curious as to what this man striding toward them had in mind, but they were not intimidated. Not a lot of the villagers, if any, had ever walked up to them so courageously in the many places they had visited and terrorized. It was rare and more than just a little interesting.

"Welcome to our village. Is there anything we can do for you?" Abe Neufeld blurted out, speaking more quickly and less calmly than he had hoped. The horsemen laughed. "We can provide you with food and a meal if you are seeking sustenance," Neufeld ventured, suddenly aware that he may have made a huge mistake stepping into the middle of this swarm of men, who were very possibly drunk, who were always unpredictable, explosively irrational and dangerous beyond reason.

Laughing again, "We're not interested in what you want to give us, you fat shithead," one of the younger men answered. The others chortled. "We only want what we take, and we take what we want." More guffaws followed. Molosovich spat on the ground.

"I did not come out to argue with you. I come as a neighbour respecting you and offering you our hospitality."

"You're not our fucking neighbour and we don't want your religious hospitality," bellowed another rider just back of Molosovich. He, their leader, said nothing, apparently amused by the encounter, but probably curious as to what might happen next.

"And you're not a comrade either, whatever the hell that is!" hooted a man at the back of the group. "You're not Russian, you're a German scum dog. You've skinned us Russians for too long and the time has come for us to finally have something." The speaker spat like his leader and looked to his comrades for assent and encouragement.

Neufeld's dog moved away from his master's side and sniffed at the front leg of one of the horses. He noticed now that every one of the men on horseback had a rifle, of sorts. He hoped, as was sometimes the case, that none of them had any ammunition. Out here in Siberia guns were often just a show of force, or at best, just a club. As the dog sniffed at the hoof of one of the horses he startled it, and the horse bolted sideways, almost unsaddling its rider. In frightened response, the dog darted toward the garden fence and its sentinel row of drying pink and red hollyhocks. With the sudden movement one of the nearest riders instantly leveled his rifle at the dog and pulled the trigger. In nearly the same instant as the sound of the rifle's shot echoed off the village buildings and reverberated down the street, the victim dog exploded. Flying fur, flesh, guts, bones and blood knocked some of the tall hollyhocks against the wooden fence; the splattering bloody red substance decorated the whitewashed pickets with its graphic horror. The people of Schönweise, hearing the gun fire, froze where they were in their kitchens, their barns, their blacksmith shops, their outhouses, and out in front of the village store. The men up the street and around the corner, already uneasy and still in their disagreement about defending themselves, but able to see through the gap in the buildings between them and the encounter on the street, started for their own homes on the run, wondering desperately now where their wives and daughters, and all their children, might be. Peter Reimer, determined now to get his gun, scrambled down the dusty street toward his parent's home.

Abe Neufeld stood still. He was determined to not let these men see that they could intimidate or dissuade him from his intention of talking them down from whatever horror plan they were hatching. But his heart was racing, he could feel it beating against the inside of his coat, the blood was up in his face. He did not let himself think about his dog. He knew that any show of anger or fear would quickly scuttle his cause. He knew, too, intuitively, that whatever would happen in the very next seconds would determine whatever it was that would occur over the next half hour or more. Anything was possible. Time stopped.

But the dog-killing gunshot had frightened fifteen-year-old Katie Doerksen out of the Günther home and foolishly (how could she know what was prudent?) she scooted out the front door past the horseman and Abe Neufeld standing with them in the street, all in a panicky attempt to get to her own home and family in the direction of the store. "Oh no," Neufeld cried silently deep inside himself, and maybe he even screamed, he was never able to remember afterwards, as one of the horsemen spurred his horse after the running teenager.

The horsemen did not know it, but Neufeld did, that Katie had at least ten of the wooden and sod houses to get past to get to her own home. Neufeld thought, in a flash of awareness while she made her first few steps, "at least they're not shooting her," but the rider caught up to the running Katie at about the third house gate, and leaning over he deftly reached down off his moving horse and scooped her up off the ground. He dropped her face down across the horse in front of his saddle, turned the animal in a quick yank of the reins and headed for the outer edge of the village. Katie was kicking and screaming and twisting to try to get herself off the speeding horse. The rider had one hand down hard on her back in front of him. The girl's face was dangerously close to the pumping front shoulder and upper leg of the horse on one side as it was spurred up the street, her feet were wildly kicking up and out on the other. One of her shoes flew off. As the abductor galloped past his brothers in arms they nodded to each other, clicked "Giddup!" to their horses, and simply followed their evil companion. Molosovich had a small smile on his face.

Katie's screams were heard throughout the whole western side of Schönweise; its people distractedly busied themselves by digging into whatever emotional semblance of safety they could find to drown out the screams, sure that their world was finally spinning violently out of control. Some of the people prayed; others, especially those closest to Katie, could not, they were too distressed.

When it was clear that the monstrous men had really left the confines of the village, a group of men and women left their homes and ran to those already in the school building and church to join in the praying. Peter Reimer, by this time back on the street with his rifle in hand, frantically pleaded for the men, the older teenagers, anyone, absolutely anyone, to join him in chasing after the brigands. Jasche Loewen, back on the street as well, shouted at Peter, in essence repeating what he had said before, "It is better to pray, Peter! And believe!"

No one volunteered to join David's home militia. He sat down on the street, leaned against the store and wept, cradling his old rifle. He knew its chambers contained no bullets; he had none. He could muster no help for his war; he had never felt so powerless.

Katie's best friend, Lena Günther, and the children in the last house of the village said they heard Katie screams coming up from the tree bluffs just outside the village for a long time that evening. Many years later Lena would say she could still hear Katie whenever her mind and reluctant memories flooded back to that day.

Without any words of argument among themselves the men of Schönweise set out as early as they dared move into the rising light of the coming sun to find Katie the next morning. They found her lying like a broken doll in the bush at the edge of town. Her twisted and bleeding body was some hundred metres or so from the crossroads between Schönweise and the Jewish *shtetl* down the road; the men were surprised to find her still alive. They had been sure that they would find only a body. Many of them had spent the entire night with the Doerksens. Miraculously, maybe — or maybe not — Katie was still alive. Breathing, yes, but whether her spirit would ever recuperate would only be known in time, so great was the damage done to her by the marauding human beasts. Not surprisingly it was Abe Neufeld who carried her limp body back to the Doerksen home. There the strong women of the village took over her care. The village doctor, not a trained doctor, but one who had read and studied much about medicines and healing, and Grandma Heide, the community's self-educated naturopath and *chnibbler* set to caring for Katie with the other attending women. They bathed Katie with warm soapy water and spoke soothingly to her; they gently touched her broken body, and maybe even her soul in their caring. Some held her at times, kissed her on the forehead, and sometimes they held and rocked her. Katie was silent. She did not cry. Her eyes were wide open. They seemed to see nothing. The deacons of the church organized a prayer meeting specifically for her and for her family. When the word went out about the prayer meeting for her and her family, someone asked if they would pray, too, for her tormentors, after all, they needed prayer, they did not yet have salvation, as Katie already did. The deafening silence from the gathered people of Schönwiese in response to the question as to whether the perpetrators of the crime should be prayed for felt like the only act of aggression remaining that should have been extended to the brigands before they carried poor Katie away.

Peter Reimer, impotent gun still in hand, paced in the street. He suggested a community meeting to the men standing in small huddles and bunches in front of the Doerksen home, but the response was less than enthusiastic. The men

DANNY UNRAU

did, though, keep glancing down the main street of the village to its borders watching for who and what might happen next. Not one suggested that someone contact the Russian police in Barnaul. They knew that would make no difference. No one would come. No official seemed to care about outrages such as this, not in the Mennonite villages, and even less in the Jewish *shtetls*.

Molosovich and his band had left their encampment sometime during the night and when the older boys went to look there were only remnants of their presence, a few empty bottles, the ashes of a camp-fire, food wastes, and a girl's shoe. The trampled grass and numerous mounds of horse feces signalled they had remained for some hours. Obviously they had felt no danger in lingering near the village. They may not have known themselves whether they would ever come back. Most of them probably would not even remember that they had been in Schönweise. Katie and her family, and the villagers, however, would never forget. Even in a new land a long way away and a long time after, they would remember. A few would be able to talk about this horror then, most would not.

Chapter 7
Stuttgart, Germany — 1970

Ben Ruhe, now twenty, and spending a year away from home, was sweeping the street out in front of the Willemshof Seniors Home and Retreat Centre where he was working as a volunteer. Each business establishment was responsible for keeping the road running past its property clean to the centre line of the road. The street snaking its way past Willemshof was a near highway; the Mercedes and the BMWs and even the French Peugeots and the diminutive Deux Chevauxs screamed along it at high speeds. Anyone cleaning and sweeping the road here at its highest peak between valleys right where it passed Willemshof literally took their lives in their hands. Beyond being amazed at how fastidious his German hosts were in their need for cleanliness, Ben thought it was all so ridiculous to be sweeping anything at this point on the road because any dust swept up by the broom got caught in the slipstream of speeding cars and blown all over the place before it was tamed against the curb and shoveled up for decent disposal anyway. That the bus stopped immediately in front of the retreat centre only served to increase the chances of serious auto accidents, or someone on the road like himself being run over.

Willemshof was home to some sixty retirees or so and staffed by a half dozen "nuns" or deaconesses of the Mennonite variety, all in black and white habit, and another dozen cleaning and kitchen staff, all women. The rare male around the place was the administrator, Adolf, who ruled the place with an iron fist. Why he saw himself as a sergeant major in this pastoral place, no one knew, there were no slackers or rebels on staff who needed to be motivated or bullied to do their work. Maybe his name had embittered him, or maybe it was in his case as has been said about Karl Marx, that he was so sour about life because "he had boils on his bum."

Willemshof was a true German establishment; sparkling cleanliness was a given. The kitchen was washed down by six people every Friday, all moving completely around the room and each covering the other's clean tracks to make sure the place was clean beyond a doubt. The institution's car was taken out of the garage every Saturday morning and washed and vacuumed according to a tightly prescribed plan, clearly diagrammed for anyone who might want to know, whether it had been moved and driven since last Saturday's cleaning or not. For there not to have been any newly settled dust on the car since week's cleaning gave Willemshof's eccentric and decidedly joyless custodian, Otto, great satisfaction, but never did it deter him from ordering anyone he thought he might have some authority over in his department that it be washed and cleaned again just like last week, all according to the plan, of course.

One Saturday, the Canadian volunteer, Ben, another rare male on the premises and the lone worker at Willemshof not socialized in things German, and therefore less persuaded about the required cleanliness of the place, was sweeping, lackadaisically. He was following the orders of the unsmiling, Otto, and indirectly the demands of the grim Adolf, but at the same time he was watching for speeding cars coming up the hill like bullets toward him, and for anything less dangerous that might distract him from this mindless and seemingly meaningless work. He saw the *Post Bus* winding its way up the hill toward him. He stepped up onto the curb to allow it room to pull up to the stop and unload its passengers. A young lady got off. Their eyes met. And locked. She with her sophisticated European but casual dress, mid-calf length skirt with matching pullover in a subtle plum and correspondingly coloured shoes, and he with his North American quasi-hippie, tie-dyed T-shirt, sandals and wildly askew, shoulder length hair stood in huge contrast to one another but it would have been noted, though, to anyone who might have seen them, that something like electricity flew between them in the second they were frozen together, two metres apart. He with broom in hand, she surprised that someone was standing there as if to welcome her off the bus. The young woman turned away after the bus pulled away from the curb, stepped across the road, checking to make sure no car was speeding her way — she knew this place — and headed down the hill on the other side of the street, looking back over her shoulder once. Then again. Her walk shouted confidence and energy. She knew she was being watched by the street sweeper, and her body language signalled that she liked it. Ben made no move to hide that he was watching her. Boredom and unused testosterone are dangerous partners in crime and stupidity. Something more than what usually strikes a young man in seeing an attractive young woman for the first time struck him about her. That she seemed to reciprocate his notice did not discourage him either.

"Wow!" he said, aloud. "She must be Walter Becker's daughter," he thought. Ben had heard that farmer Becker, whose large and progressive farming operation was just down the road from Willemshof, and who sat on the Board of Directors of the centre, had a daughter studying in Munich. It was rumored that the daughter did not, as it were, buy into many of the family Becker's values, and certainly not into her father's religious thinking. She was an outspoken intellectual, he had heard, with many interests and passions. She was reputed to be some kind of student radical with strong leftist leanings. And as if differences over theology and philosophy were not enough, she was known to be openly critical and very outspoken about her father having served with the Nazis during the war, even though she knew it had been rumoured that he had done something quite extraordinary before the war ended. She knew that he had served at Dachau, and she could not get past his refusal to speak to her of anything of those fascist days and what his experience had been. Whether it was just a political thing between the two, or a daughter yearning for an intimate father-daughter relationship she did not know and probably would not have been conscious of at that time. The next generation would ask that question.

Ben smiled as he swept the rest of the dust off the pavement. A beautiful girl to look at on a lazy afternoon being filled with needless work was a sublime treat. In temperament, he was something of a lone wolf though he could be very extroverted, and for the first time in his life he was open to any adventure that might come his way, even one he would probably never consider at home. He had grown up in a fairly strict environment, morals well proscribed, but now, he was largely unaware that some of the rules of his upbringing and previous existence were, if not on hold, at least unlocking and opening to being tested. Ready for negotiation. He was succumbing almost as carelessly as he swept, to a devil-may-care attitude as he moved from childhood to adulthood, testing the edges of his values looking to discover his own authenticity as a person.

Nevertheless, Ben thought little more of the young lady with the jaunty walk and the confident stride away from him toward the estate down the hill. One of the Sisters came and asked him to carry something to her room for her. He liked Sister Liza, the mischievous nun. He had read once that every convent has at least one nun who is a little more frolicsome than the others, and in Willemshof it was Liza. He was always glad to give the elderly saint a hand. She made him laugh, and he made her laugh. They had entered into a wordless social contract to always laugh together. In their unique friendship they had agreed to shake loose the religious dourness that had permeated their respective formative years of faith and this place where they both now lived.

The supper bell rang somewhere deep in the main building of Willemshof. Supper time had finally arrived. Ben found his place at the table among the female workers gathering for the meal. One of the domestic volunteers was a pregnant girl sent to Willemshof to avoid the whispers in her community until the baby was born. She tried to hate Ben and fired verbal insults his way every chance she got, which he easily deflected. Another kitchen worker was a cute French girl named Monique who knew the art of flirtation to a fault. Here in the mini-dining room the nuns and the rest of the staff ate their weekday meals. There was always an interesting dynamic in the room.

Stern Mother Superior Liesel called out to Ben, after a solemn table grace for the meal was spoken, to tell him that the neighbour Herr Becker had called. The Becker sons and their sister were going to the circus in the city that night and the boys were wondering whether he wanted to go along. Ben's heart skipped a beat remembering his random meeting with the Becker daughter at the bus stop earlier that day. He did not know, as he coolly thanked Sister Liesel and replied that he would be happy to go to the circus with the Beckers, that his life was about to take an interesting and, for a time, exciting turn.

Martin, the youngest Becker son, came to the Ben's door after dinner as arranged to say they were ready to leave for the circus. The travelling circus troupe from Italy was decidedly less than impressive as a circus, but soon it appeared not to matter. Ben and the Becker daughter, the young woman who had gotten off the bus earlier in the day, and so jauntily walked away from Ben, leaning on his broom beside the road, were quickly becoming acquainted. The spark that might have been between them at first sight had not dimmed; it was in fact, igniting. As the Becker brothers exchanged glances and rolled their eyes through the circus event, Ben and Liesbett, as he quickly learned was her name, laughed and talked and flirted shamelessly, their interaction became the main performance under the big tent that evening. They discovered similar interests and, predictably, compared notes as to their personal schedules over the next few days.

The next day Ben knocked on the door of a student resident studio apartment at the University Hospital to which Liesbett had just transferred and was living, studying and working. Smiling and happy, they became better acquainted. Promises of a destiny together hung in the air as they found hours to spend together.

When Herr Becker heard that his daughter was spending time with the Willemshof volunteer from Canada, he attempted to exercise his considerable Germanic parental power upon Liesbett. But Liesbett was not easily overpowered. Not even by a father with strict and traditional Mennonite sensibilities, nor even with the seldom mentioned but real Nazi experience in his past. As for Ben, the more Liesbett lamented the negatives her father placed upon her for the time she was spending with him, the more intensely he felt about this young woman teaching him things he had not known: emotions and passions. Only later would he realize that his attraction for her was in direct proportion to her father's displeasure of him. Had Herr Becker not shown so much negative concern, Ben would have probably drifted away fairly soon. He and Liesbett were too different; Ben felt the relationship becoming all too complicated for him almost immediately. Guilt for his feelings of ambivalence toward her while still engaging in the relationship was also working its way into his conscience. A few thousand miles away from his home and its deep-seated morality was not distant enough away to let the young Mennonite man run rampant like the sixties free spirit he sometimes wanted to be, or pretended to be. But as her father persisted in pressuring Liesbett to cease and desist in her relationship with the *Kanadier*, Ben kept articulating his affection for her and his sympathy that she had such a bullying dad, who had, after all, been a Nazi.

Liesbett told Ben about her involvement with the *Sozialistischer Deutscher Studentenbund*, a leftist student group with ties to the *Baader-Meinhof Gruppe*, a notorious radical German urban terrorist group, itself loosely aligned with the Japanese Red Guard and philosophically connected to Angela Davis and the Black Panthers in the United States. Liesbett became impassioned as she talked about having helped a political prisoner break out of jail in Berlin and gain political asylum in Cuba. Ben told Liesbett she was crazy, and commented, tongue in cheek, that life in Castro's Cuba was undoubtedly a paradise. He would hold forth with a twinkle in his eye and the passion of a TV preacher that life is about "Peace and love, man."

Ben would smile in the face of Liesbett's appeal to the seriousness of her passions stating that the hippie-peace world he was only dabbling on the edge of was no less dysfunctional than the world she was playing in, but at least it had some good intentions. "My dream world has no intention of hurting anyone, even if it sometimes does. Your political world finds people expendable, in fact, finds way to eradicate them," he would tell her. "Mine doesn't!"

Liesbett was puzzled. It seemed he was more interested in listening to the music of Cat Stevens and Donovan, and more annoyed about having missed out on Woodstock the year before back home on Yasgur's farm in Bethel, New York, than the injustices in the world. She knew he had worked in high rise construction in Canada that summer to earn money to travel around Europe, all of which resulted in their meeting, but it had been a long time since she had a friend who was so disinterested in intellectual politics and East-West issues. Liesbett was both repulsed and drawn by Ben's political apathy and his naïveté; sometimes, she said she wished life could be as carefree and playful as he seemed to make it. It was clear to her that he had neither financial and family means, nor the education and drive to "get anywhere," but none of that seemed to matter to him. He was not foolhardy nor even reckless, like many students she knew, he was certainly bright and aware, showing some interest in these important matters, but somehow he refused to be nonplussed by so much of the world and what was, or was not going on. Ironically, this mystery about him just made him more attractive to her. She wanted to teach him, run away with him, love him, spit at him, and hate him all at the same time. She was strangely hooked. And he was along for an adventure, an experience. That she could tell. Liesbett felt that he was using her but it also felt like he cared for her. Ben did care for her. He liked her. He liked her mind. He was even attracted to her passion for politics, her sense of justice and the need for reform in the world, though he was bemused by its supremacy in her thinking, her singlemindedness. "There's so much more, Liesbett. The world is bigger than politics," he would say to her as she handed him articles in complicated German that he could hardly read. "There are deeper things: spiritual realities, emotional issues, family dynamics. Politics is only one of the panels on your European *fussballs*, Liesbett, don't get too carried away. And your conservative, right-wing dad, is right, I'm no good!" he grinned.

These conversations infuriated her. And drew her in. If he wanted to capture her he was doing the right thing. He was not malicious enough, however, to deliberately manipulate her. Perhaps it was all little more than two young people maybe a little in love, a lot foolish and somehow hooked.

It was after one of their confusing conversations that Liesbett could hardly tell whether he cared or did not care, about her or her ideas, that she told him that her student group was planning a trip to Berlin and the Soviet Union. Ben perked up his ears. Suddenly he was more serious. He had already told her that his parents and grandparents, his people, came from Russia. Something in his search for identity sparked into being when Liesbett talked about going to Russia, and in the hint that he might be invited to go along.

Chapter 8
36,000 feet over the Atlantic – 1990

A gaggle of Hasidic men and a pair of Orthodox Jews of another stripe gathered at the back of the El Al plane. They took up most of the narrow galley, blocked the flight attendants needing to serve their customers, and filled all of the exit space at the rear door as well. It was morning prayer time. The pray-ers got busy donning their *tefillin*, winding the leather straps meticulously around their arms and foreheads so that the tiny texts of the Torah inside the leather boxes would be close to their hearts, on their forearms, and next to their minds as the biblical injunctions and centuries old commentary had instructed them to do. Then, facing Jerusalem as best they could from an airplane travelling at 36,000 feet and six-hundred miles an hour, they commenced their prayers, *davening* books in hand. Long side curls swung to and fro as the pious pray-ers rhythmically bobbed back and forth, bending at their waists, their bodies fully engaged in praying, exhibiting their sincere belief that prayer is not only verbal and spiritual but physical as well. Everything in these men entered into their praying. They flipped through the pages of their prayer books, not missing a beat of their religious ritual. Flight attendants needing to get to their tasks in the galley, or trying to get to items in the exit space, were resigned to the imposition placed upon them by the worshippers and they seemed unperturbed by this sacred intrusion. They had seen and been through this dance many times before. This was, after all, El Al, Israel's national airline. Things Jewish could be expected on these flights. The flight attendants knew there was no chance of changing the minds or the behaviour of the pray-ers, and had probably been told early in their training to make no effort to do so.

The pray-ers, in turn, completely ignored the flight attendants going about their business in and around them. Secular Jews, which most of the El Al flight attendants would be, always insisted they harboured no ill will against the religious element of the broader Jewish community, whether they were praying in public places, throwing stones at theatres and stores doors and windows when operators opened the doors too soon at the end of a Sabbath, or stopping cars driving too early on Saturday evenings. Such pious, watch-care behaviour, they mused, kept the entire nation of Israel and the Jewish people of the world to a certain level of righteousness.

Driven by his inability to sit for long periods, his sociability and his abiding interest in things Jewish, Ben Ruhe stepped into the middle of the praying circle and began praying too. His prayer partners had no idea that his prayers were "in the name of *Jeshuah!*" After all, he smiled within himself, his Messiah was as Jewish as these men were. He realized a moment or two into his own praying that he too had unconsciously begun bobbing his head back and forth in rhythm with his unwitting prayer partners.

The enthusiasm and vigour of the pray-ers in their praying rose and fell throughout the time of their ritual. All the while, and in between, conversations between the worshippers took place as well. While deeply serious in their practice, these were not mystics who fell into a trance and lost connection with their world or the people around them. Prayers and conversations with fellow pray-ers flowed in and out of one another without barriers and boundaries. Periods of intensity in bobbing and weaving were bracketed by less enthusiastic movement interspersed with mutterings for a few moments, eventually waned to the point of silence. Having completed their morning prayers and kissed their prayer books, the men gave themselves over to more conversation as they carefully and affectionately wrapped and folded their phylacteries into their special pouches. The sharing of news and views, with not a little disagreement over some issue to which the Torah, the Hebrew texts and the ancient rabbis had already spoken to evoked discussion and energy. Any observer uninitiated in the ways of Jewish study and discourse would have thought the men were at each others' throats; in actual fact, the discussion was rather low key compared to most in any synagogue or place of Jewish study, it being early in the day and the men probably more interested to pass the time on this long flight than end once and for all an ancient never-ending discussion.

Ben moved in as closely to the group as he dared, some of its members still concluding their prayers as others lingered to talk, trying to get the gist of the energized conversation that was being conducted in a mixture of Hebrew, English and Yiddish, hoping even to get involved if possible. The men, young and not-so young, some bearded, some not, wearing wide brimmed fedoras over knitted or more formal black *yarmulkes* in their black suits, tie-less white shirts, long knotted tassels hanging down over the waistbands of their trousers, could have been from anywhere Jews live in the world. Their dress was a kind of religious Jewish uniform, not so notable, yet clearly recognizable as to a particular people's faith and identity. Not vastly unlike, Ben thought to himself, some of the more conservative Mennonite and Amish groups he had seen in various parts of the world.

Ben was a non-entity in this crowd. If he were viewed as Jewish in the circle, he would be seen to be a secular Jew wearing none of the usual religious trappings. His gentle intrusion into the group seemed not to be resented. In fact, it was as if he were not present at all. Soon he was able to strike up a conversation with a gentleman who appeared to be somewhere between sixty and seventy years old. Before long the two of them were enthusiastically exchanging stories — stories of youth and family, work and, of course, religion and faith.

Daveed, an Orthodox Jew, but not Hasidic in practice, told Ben that he had been a banker with Bank Hapoalim in Toronto but was on his way home to retirement in Jerusalem. Ben reported that he was a one-time teacher, and now a Christian clergyman with a graduate degree in Judaism, on his way to Jerusalem to lead a tour of pilgrims through the Holy Land, and then, hopefully, to conduct some research for a book. Ben added that he and his wife had worked on a kibbutz in the *Galil* in their honeymoon year and he was, of course, hoping to reconnect with some of the *kibbutzniks* he had made lifelong friendships with.

"You are so interested in things Jewish?" Daveed remarked, more a question than a statement.

"Yes!" came Ben's response.

"But why?"

"Why not?"

"It's not usual!"

"It's not that uncommon for Christians to be interested in Jews and Judaism and Israel," Ben countered, having learned some skills of Jewish exchange and argument replete with the right rhythm and singsong, raising his voice at the end of each sentence with a tone that implies it should all be so obvious to the other person.

"Oh, but it is! No one in the world is curious about us much beyond pushing us into the sea," retorted the banker.

"I think you are wrong there, but my writing, my research, is more personal," said Ben.

"And what is the nature of your research?"

"Actually I'm writing a story about a young man, a devoted follower of the Jewish Jeshuah, who after years of attempting to authentically live and practice his Christian faith discovers he has Jewish roots, that there is Jewish blood in his ancestry, and with such a discovery goes through a deep identity crisis. He finds that he needs to revisit and re-discover who he is and what it is that faith and religion mean to him. In short, his historical and theological self-image takes a hit and he begins a spiritual and religious search for himself."

"Is this a book or an article you are writing?"

"It's a book, I think, a novel, so that where I cannot find actual historical fact I can speculate as to what might have happened in the lives of the characters."

"Is your novel autobiographical?"

"Oh no," Ben laughed. "I have no Jewish blood in me. My people are longstanding Christians. Protestants. Mennonites, in fact, with a rich history of faith, and persecution, that runs back to Russia, Prussia, Switzerland and the Netherlands, right back to the sixteenth century reformation. The Mennonites, although, you might be interested to know, have often claimed that the movie *A Fiddler On the Roof* is as much their story as it is a Jewish story. But, no, my book's not autobiographical in any way."

"But you said you have friends in Tel Aviv, you're leading tours in the land, you've lived and studied in Jerusalem, you have a graduate degree in Judaism?"

"Yes!"

"And in your honeymoon year you came and worked on a kibbutz in the *Galill*?"

"Yes!"

"You are the boy!"

"What boy?"

"You are the boy you are writing about in the book. You cannot excuse yourself. No Christian comes and works on a kibbutz, comes back and studies Judaism, takes people on tour through the land, and loves Israel the way you seem to do just because. It doesn't happen. You are the boy."

"I have no Jewish ancestors. I have no Jewish blood. I am not the boy. This is all your imagination," Ben exclaimed emphatically.

"One day, one day, my dear young friend, you will discover that somewhere in your past is a Jewish mother, probably one of your grandmothers. The life, the forces you describe within yourself as having do not come just out of curiosity; it is much deeper. You are the boy. The Christian who discovers he is a Jew and then has to do something about it. You are the boy!" Daveed insisted. Ben laughed. He waved his hand and shrugged his shoulders not unlike a Jew who had just lost an argument but knowing there is always another day to continue it.

When Ben disembarked from the plane on the tarmac at Ben Gurion Airport in Tel Aviv some hours later, he repressed an overwhelming urge to kiss the ground at the bottom of the boarding ramp. Others around him were doing so. He stopped himself, feeling foolish for wanting to, and feeling disloyal for not doing so.

Days later when he stepped out of a bus on the Mount of Olives having travelled south along the west bank of the Jordan River from Tiberias before coming up from Jericho to this spot above the Holy City, he was surprised by his emotions. As he drank in the stunning panoramic view of the city of Jerusalem after a lifetime of immersed study of the Bible and nearly a twenty year absence from this powerfully mystical and spiritual city, he could not hold back the tears. He wept. His mind went to the New Testament account of Jesus weeping at probably very nearly the same spot wishing he could gather this city into himself *"like a hen gathers her brood of chicks under her wings,"* feeling deep love, sadness, fear, affection, and connection, all at the same time.

Chapter 9
Berlin/Moscow/Yaroslav, USSR — 1971

The train bound for Berlin slipped out of Stuttgart before six in the morning, carrying among its many passengers some serious students on a mission. Middle-class, well-to-do, intellectual, ideological students with socialistic leanings who were more than just a little interested in political studies. They could not hide their excitement that they were finally on their "political Hajj" bound for their own kind of Mecca, the Soviet Union. While most in the group were self-proclaimed political junkies and purists of the Marxist-Leninist variety, Liesbett had been allowed to invite Ben to go along, although she did not tell her comrades the depth of his often expressed cynicism about the group's political leanings and proclivities.

"I can stand almost anywhere politically if it means a trip somewhere," Ben had laughed one evening taking aim at her seriousness and unabashedly admitting his appetite to travel to as many places in the world as he possibly could, as if he were filling a book shelf with books to make himself look like a man with a library. She had wondered aloud about his integrity, and her own, in him being part of this junket. Liesbett did not feel overly safe with Ben's a-political swagger and was concerned what he might blurt out, or might do, when he was with her travelling companions. She tried to make it clear to him that the Cold War, clearly and completely the fault of the western so-called democratic powers, most notably the imperialistic United States and its friends, including West Germany, was still significantly frosty, and these students, she reminded him, were very much impressed by, and in favour of the Soviet socialist experiment before they even got there. She had said all this with a "and you better believe it and behave!" tone in her voice.

"Whatever!" Ben laughed. He attended two planning meetings with the group a few weeks before the onset of the trip. He was not a student of politics by any stretch of the imagination, compared to these garrulous German students. They worked too hard, he thought, to make the longest possible sentences from the biggest words they could muster "like artists at an exhibition" all for show, and their Marxism seemed intellectual rather than practical. They could afford to be stridently socialist, he told Liesbett, for they would always have enough and more coming from the upper middle class situations they were in and the families they were a part of in a comfortable West Germany. He told some of them that, too, though he tried not to overstate his cynicism about their political opinions. They were not offended. They thought he was just trying to be humorously provocative for sport. And perhaps it was good they did not take him too seriously; he was not interested in jeopardizing and souring this chance of a trip to his parents' homeland.

Finally the travelling road show to political utopia was on the train. Ben had not actually purchased the tickets for his trip; at every point of departure they were handed to him when needed. When he had asked what the trip would cost at various junctures of the planning, he was always informed that the group's trip was covered mostly by a grant, and he should not worry. So he did not, and upon later reflection suspected that political interests, maybe even the Communist Party somewhere, perhaps in Russia or East Germany itself, had paid for his junket. He hoped so. It would be some sweet revenge for the horrors the Soviet communists had visited upon his people in parts of the Soviet Union and Siberia some fifty years earlier, and in its longer history.

The Moscow bound tour stopped in Berlin for a few days, where the participants were given extensive tours of the "successful" East zone. They walked through Checkpoint Charlie, one of the infamous crossing points between West and East Berlin, *Vopos* stared down their gun sights and through binoculars at them from their ominous watch-towers as the student-tourists "crossed over" into East Berlin. They took long stairways angling down below the drastically divided city streets of this great German city to the S-Bahn, and enthusiastically entered the *Staatsoper* on *Unter den Linden Strasse* in East Berlin; all a grand tour of the high lights of a city desperate to be taken seriously for more reasons than the obvious. The members of this tour group with the clothes and the benefits of the West, with convictions they thought made them political and social siblings and kindred spirits with those on the "truly" democratic and eastern side of the Wall, were guided like special guests and given VIP treatment by their hosts.

Ben had been in East Berlin on his own a few months earlier. He had almost been roughed up and arrested by some East German policemen with no sense of humour when he was seen not so respectfully photographing another reckless Canadian who had suddenly jumped onto the lap of the enormous sculpted Russian soldier at the Soviet War Memorial in Treptower Park to plant a kiss on its huge metal lips. Ben found East Berlin to be dark and dingy, backward and depressed, and in spirit, cold and unfriendly. He could not be sure, but he suspected great fear was abiding in the people of this eastern portion of the city. None of his travel mates on this visit, however, seemed to notice what he noticed, nor could they agree with him when he shared his observations that the people on the streets and in the service establishments of East Berlin were no true, ideological communists. They seemed to him more a people intimidated and downtrodden — victims of an institutionalized fear and a well organized system of confining repression.

After their scheduled days in Berlin, the travellers boarded an Aeroflot plane bound for Moscow. Excitement among the pilgrims ran high as they anticipated seeing the Soviet socialist system in resounding action. Ben was excited, too, not for political reasons, but for the opportunity to see something of — to actually be in — the land of his forefathers. He felt, certainly for the first time at such depth, profound connection to his own roots, to the people who had fled the Soviet Union because its communist system had failed to protect what they had been promised by ways of rights and freedoms a hundred and fifty years earlier, especially the right to freely expressed faith and to never have to bear arms in the military. He remembered the stories his father and uncles recounted how the increasingly godless Soviet authorities had not protected Mennonite villages from the ravages of travelling bands of hooligans, anarchists and miscreants who respected no persons, nor any laws. Ben knew of the thousands who had disappeared into the Gulag and of those who had left Russia, most notably his own relatives in the 1920s, to make their way to Canada, South America, Mexico and the United States. He could not recall that anyone ever expressed anything less than a sense of liberation and freedom and enormous relief to get out of the political and military spiritual hellhole first created by Vladimir Lenin, then sustained by Josef Stalin.

While Ben had been spiritually and socially nurtured by quiet, mostly peace loving Mennonite people, it was always made clear in the storytelling of his family circle that the communist regime of the modern Soviet Union was nothing less than evil, and its leaders, evil incarnate. Often his mostly gentle relatives talked with great affection for Russia, its deep, rich, soil, and the incredible opportunity that it had once promised them as a people. In the end, they were quick to say, they left was what had become anti-religious, devilish, corrupt, and destructive to all but the very few at the top of the system; dangerous and deadly to even most of its own people, and the whole world.

Ben remembered tearful prayers of thanksgiving in Canadian Mennonite homes for having been allowed, by God's hand, to emigrate. He could still hear in his memory passionate prayers of intercession for those still behind the Iron Curtain uttered every Sunday and Wednesday in their churches, or whenever they gathered as a praying people.

Ben was not about to embrace the positively charged emotions of his new friends, agog with Moscow as if it were some kind of fantastic political and social wonderland. His own identity and bond with a divergent and different perspective was far too deep. He was beginning to understand that who each human is has long roots into the past about which the individual can do little but discover, attempt to understand, sort, file, expunge and delete where necessary, and hopefully, then nurture and celebrate.

The tour group, upon arrival in Moscow, took up residence in the Intourist Hotel on the bank of the Moskva River. During the days of their visit they toured the Moscow University, attended by students reportedly at no cost to them, the Technology and Science Exhibition Park, the Gum Department Store, and, of course, Lenin's tomb with the revolutionist's embalmed body enshrined in plexiglass purportedly refusing to decay like a biblical Holy One. Ben was often surrounded by Russian school students wanting to give him pins of the Soviet bear and the hammer and the sickle. Often, once they found out he was a Canadian, he engaged in friendly arguments with the youngsters about who the real hockey power of the world was: Canada or Russia? How could any of them know that the 1972 Summit Series and a humble player by the name of Paul Henderson would settle that argument once and for all as Canada and Russia waged hockey war?

Evenings during their stay in Moscow, Ben would sometimes slip away from the hotel and go for surreptitious walks with blackmarketeers on the bridge over the famous river. On one of these walks he sold half of his two-blue-jeans wardrobe for 90 Russian roubles, a political act more than an economic one, in the end, when he found he could not take the roubles out of the country when the tour was over anyway.

On a Sunday morning, Ben found himself curious about and wanting to find a Mennonite Church in Moscow to somehow connect spiritually and emotionally with his past and his family back home. This was spiritual and emotional, an unintentional pull, new to him after some teenage years of trying to distance himself from his roots. With two fellow travellers he had to settle for a large Baptist Church meeting-house that the taxi driver would only drop them off a block away from for fear of being seen near a church. When the three young people gained seats in the upper balcony of the church for the service, Ben thought he heard spiritual moanings and longings reminiscent of his parents' sentimental stories of life in the bosom of Mother Russia. He felt a spiritual connection with his people in that church that morning though he could understand nothing of the language. Something stirred within him at the service. He wondered later that day what this force within him might be; years later he would know.

Two days later the tour travelled north across the Russian Plain with its shrubbery and swamplands to Yaroslav on the Volga River and on to Rostov on Lake Nero to stay in a marvellous compound that had once been a Russian Orthodox monastery dating back to the twelfth century. The purpose of the centre, and this gathering, was to bring together Russian youth and young people from western nations who were sympathetic to the Soviet experiment. Ben was introduced to the children and grandchildren, all his own age, of highly ranked Soviet Communist Party members. One young Russian woman, blonde and beautiful, attractive enough to grace the cover of any western fashion magazine became very friendly. Ben was hesitant, confused, caught between his loyalty to Liesbett and his intrigue in the newness and the aura of mystery around the young Russian woman. He sensed the possibility of history repeating itself between the two of them. But he was suddenly cautious, even a little shy. Had their respective grandparents met somewhere in this vast land? He imagined the young woman's grandfather somehow responsible for the harrowing train ride out of the country nearly fifty years ago that his grandfathers had taken, and barely survived. For once, he was mostly silent. He asked few questions of the young woman and her friends. Wells of feelings and questions hitherto unknown to him stirred; and the sensings seemed spiritual. Even Liesbett noticed. There was a change in him, a look in his eyes, she told him, in this monastery and whenever they were in a church, ancient or modern, she added. She perceived a coming change in their relationship; he may have as well.

Unwittingly his relationship with Liesbett was an aberration in the life of Ben; she was a victim of his being a long way from home and a long way away from the controls and restraints, the cautions, the good sense and thoughtfulness of his upbringing. He was thousands of miles away from ever being found out for anything he was doing. And now this journey into the heart of Russia had yanked him emotionally and spiritually back into the heartbeat of his own people. His largely unknown familial past. He could not shake the notion that his grandfathers might have come to the doors of a monastery such as this to sell their produce, to sew the monks' clothes. Perhaps they had ploughed the fields around the hermitage. It was the first time in Ben's young years that he sensed such deep connections to his past, to the ancient blood running in his veins. This was for him not a journey into Marxism-Leninism as his travelling organizers had planned; this was a journey into his own history, faith, practice and identity. This was not turning out to be some kind of political birth, it was more like a massive rebirth of a deeper order. In that communist camp housed in a former Russian Orthodox monastery, Ben realized he could not run away from what he was. He wondered, lying awake long into the night in that place, how long it would take him to get back to himself, to regain whom he had never been, but always was.

A week later the pilgrims from Germany were back on an Aeroflot flight to Berlin. Two days later Ben and Liesbett rode the train on its long winding ways back to Stuttgart. Ben had once again become uncharacteristically quiet and distant. Liesbett knew she was losing him, though she had never been completely sure she had him. She started a conversation saying that she felt that she would always be connected to him and that it felt like he was already turned toward home. Without speaking just yet the thought that he would never come back to this German existence crossed his mind. He could not yet determine whether his silencing feelings were about he and Liesbett, or about things of identity and faith, history and family connections.

"The light I see in your eyes when we are in churches and monasteries is never what I see when we discuss politics, Ben," Liesbett said looking out the window of the train watching the German villages with their red roofs flash by. Ben took her hand. "I think you will be a religious leader, maybe even a Mennonite pastor one day," she added, trying to tease, but then becoming grave again, continued, "you'll grow up to make the changes you need to become that. I'll go back to being a career nurse and a political activist on the side. I don't know if you and I could make it. Maybe both of us poured together somehow into one person could be a viable someone, but the two of us? Could we be?" Liesbett turned to him, tears in her eyes. Ben looked down at his feet, the shaking of the train causing the only movements in their bodies sitting side by side, just the two of them in the compartment. At twenty-one he could not yet distinguish between the emotions of guilt and sadness, he would have been hard pressed to clearly identify any emotions with words at that point in his life.

Two days later in Liesbett's apartment sitting on the side of her bed, and still more silent than verbal, Bob Dylan's *I Threw It all Away* playing on the record player unlocked his tears. "I'm sorry, Liesbett," he said. "I'm sorry!"

Not many days hence Ben was in New York catching a plane for Canada and home. It was time to grow up. It was time to get on with his life as he had been taught it should be, the way he now wanted it to be.

Chapter 10
White Rock, Canada — 1996

Despite never ever having considered that he might become a clergyman, Ben was in his mid thirties when he got a phone call from a minister inviting him to consider a career in the church. When a lively democratic congregation shortly thereafter invited him to be their pastor he found himself having to take seriously his belief that the collective is nearly always wiser than the individual and he yielded to the peoples wishes, and their pastor he became. There were some problems with his becoming a clergyman, however. In personal style, as a clergyman, Ben never quite knew whether he would want to be Mick Jagger-like strutting on stage "for the good of the gospel," or whether as the primary care-giver of a whole parish he should be a Mother Theresa rescuing the needy of the world with a deep and extraordinary compassion. The thing that rankled in Ben's spirit when he looked in his self-mirror was that with some authenticity he could be a bit of both. While the spirit of the sixties with which he moved through his most formative years shouted that he needed to be as consistent a person as he could be, voices of the later decades thought he might be better served as an individual if he just made some peace with his contradictions. But a clergyman Ben became and people would call him for council and companionship, advice and admonition. Distressed persons would walk through his office door and pour out their pain as he listened. They would cry and when they themselves "didn't have a prayer" he had one for them.

He was immersed in the quintessential sermon contemplating the words and meaning of *blessed are the poor in spirit* one afternoon when a young woman seemed to appear out of the shadows. He felt her presence at the door more than heard her knock. With head down and a voice barely audible, she asked permission to step over the sill and into his office. As Ben was already sitting behind his desk in his study, a disarray of papers and open books and a Bible or two before him, he just looked up without moving to stand up. She stepped into the room with his nod but then seemed to freeze just inside the door. Ben smiled and stood. He stepped around the corner of his desk toward her, thinking to welcome her and reduce her anxiety. She shrank back a step, then two, appeared to be ready to bolt and run. Ben realized his mistake and moved back to his place behind his desk trying to discern her emotion. He wondered whether they had met before, if she sat in his congregation some Sundays and now returned for an explanation or a request.

The woman was young, in her mid twenties, perhaps, though he could not be sure. Short, straight blonde hair with bangs hanging into her blue eyes framed her face. She wore sneakers and a tracksuit, black with white trim. She was neat and clean, petite and athletic, but she had a look of dishevelment about her, as if some deep disturbance was encircling her. Her eyes signalled fear. Her body was tensed and coiled, as if getting ready to run. But when Ben stopped and moved back, she came forward again, back to the spot just inside the door she had gained earlier. She sidled sideways toward the corner away from the door. "Can we talk?" she asked barely above a whisper. "Can we go in the big room?" Ben waited sensing he needed to let this nervous and frightened stranger take the lead in this encounter, or even a simple conversation between them could not or would not happen. An inner voice, one he had learned to trust, told him that this meeting mattered; that what was happening was momentous.

The seemingly socially paralyzed young woman was obviously driven by something even greater than the enormous discomfort she was experiencing just standing in the room, coming to see him, facing him but hardly able to speak. Yet she seemed to know him. As if she were in awe of him. He knew now that he had never seen her before, but he was powerfully drawn to her. He felt compassion for her. Whether it was her manifest brokenness, or something else, he could not tell.

Ben sat down. He shuffled his papers, but kept looking up as if to assure her she was welcome. He saw her take in the wall of books in his library to her right with observing eyes, then the Jewish prayer shawl on the opposite wall overlapping a Palestinian *keffiyeh* which Ben had pinned there as a kind of visible dream wish to symbolize some kind of archetypal reconciliation and peace between all enemies on earth, maybe even two faiths. She narrowed her eyes. Clearly, her mind was working to make something of this man in whose presence she now stood, whom she, for whatever reasons, had chosen to meet. She sneaked a look from the wall to the floor, and to his face, but when their eyes met, she just as quickly averted hers to some place above his head.

"What's your name?" Ben asked. His voice sounded too loud. As if he were violating the quietness she had brought into the room with her.

"I don't think I can tell you my name," she murmured. "Can we go in the big room? In the main church?" gesturing toward the wall behind his books. She seemed to know that behind the oak doors just outside Ben's office and to the left was the main sanctuary of the church of which he was the lead minister.

"Of course," he responded. He stood and started moving toward the door, motioning for her to go ahead. She froze. Ben could not recall meeting a more frightened adult. She was more than shy; she seemed nearly immobilized. Being polite and asking her to move ahead was not working, he realized in an instant and at the same moment that he needed to go ahead of her so she could follow him. She seemed unable to have anyone behind her. Ben's instincts and training as a counsellor told him she must have been hit from behind at some point in her life and had determined to never let anyone, no man, at least, ever walk behind her back. He stepped carefully around her, stayed as far away from her as he could without making it too obvious, and led the way out of his office, up the two or three steps of the landing and through the double door into the church sanctuary. The huge stained glass windows high on their left side as they entered the cavernous room filtered rich reds, blues and yellows over the burgundy pew pads and dark oak church furniture. The room was silent; it felt more sacred and still than usual for Ben. Some said that this room smelled more religious when it was empty of people, the odour of wilted flowers, burnt wax candles and hard wood faintly perceivable.

Ben sat down on the front pew closer to the door than to the centre of the large room. The perceptibly frightened, still nameless young woman moved into the row behind him, sitting down some two metres or so away from him, but still closer to the exit than where he was. Neither spoke. The huge room breathed silence. Ben waited, knowing not to talk, sensing this was a moment to wait and be silent. He had not known many moments of silence in his life; he suddenly realized he must have missed a lot from others and for himself in such unawareness. The silence lasted. One minute. Two minutes. Finally he said, "You wanted to talk. Is there something you want to say?"

"Can we just sit here for a while?" she murmured, "I think I like it here."

"Sure."

Five minutes passed. Ten minutes. Just silence. Ben's mind started to drift back to the text *blessed are the poor in spirit* he had been contemplating when the silent young woman had suddenly appeared at his door; his natural impatience and propensity to incessant activity struggling with the passivity of this encounter. He knew, though, that he had no power to evoke any conversation from her. Then he heard her whisper something. And again. He could not hear what she was saying. Ben leaned closer to her, though she was some distance away from him. He learned that doing so was a mistake. He should never move toward her.

"I think I need to go now," she said, shaking herself.

Ben nodded, careful to move toward the door in such a way that she could follow him in the direction she wanted to go, but careful to show too that she was never at risk of him getting behind her. Gaining the exit of the sanctuary, he walked slowly past his office and the other church offices, rounded the corner to the outside exit door and right out of the building onto the front sidewalk. He could hear her shuffling along, perhaps a meter or more behind him, gliding her feet flat to the floor as she followed him. Once outside on the sidewalk she hurried past him, her body turned slightly sideways away from him, her head down, her bottom lip curled under her top teeth, and reaching her car at the curb, got in, started it and drove away, seeming now to be in a hurry as if relieved to be getting away. Ben watched the car with its mystery passenger go up the street and turn the corner. He was puzzled. More than puzzled. Curious. Moved. Strangely excited, even, yet saddened, all at the same time.

Chapter 11
Jerusalem, Israel — 1998

Ben saw the group of men and women he had shown around the Holy Land for twelve days off at the Ben Gurion Airport. They told him the tour had been a resounding success. Between the intense social and religious politics of their young Palestinian bus driver and colourful Israeli tour guide, a dozen Canadian Christians with a deep interest in Biblical history and current events, and Ben with his own ties to this land — mystical and mysterious even to him — as their Mennonite clergyman leader, the experience had been exceedingly rich. Each day had been too short; each day had evoked more new questions to be asked than old ones could be answered.

With the group safely in the air after a rigorous set of questions from security officers at the airport as to whom they had all met, where they had been, why one of the group members was flying home on another day, and why he was staying on in the country, Ben found a *sherut* waiting for one more passenger for Jerusalem. The car was soon winding its way through the hills from Latrun to Bab El Wad and Castil, the memorial ruins of the tanks and trucks blown up in *Operation Nachshon* of the 1948 war still by the roadside so travellers would never forget. Riding in a car that displayed the green license plates of the Jewish sector of Jerusalem, and not the blue plates of the West Bank or the Palestinian zone, Ben and his driver were waved through the checkpoints at the western entrance to Jerusalem without a second glance from the border guards. Travelling past the Egged bus station in the west end of the city, Ben reminded the driver that he wanted to be dropped off at the Jaffa Gate. The drive through the busy city would take some time. He slipped into a reverie as they drove past Mercedes and donkeys, religious Jews in their black suits and their swinging side-curls hurrying to or from their studies, and Palestinian construction workers trying to catch buses back to their homes beyond the city and past the demeaning checkpoints.

When the car stopped outside the ancient Ottoman built Jaffa gate, Ben stepped out. He breathed in the characteristic old Jerusalem smell of strong spices in the air and donkey dung on the road, swung his knapsack with his few clothes, his personal documents, and his laptop computer over his shoulder. He walked through the ancient Jaffa Gate, making the jagged S turn of the gate itself rather than the easier direct opening made for automobiles and delivery trucks, remembering that the British General Allenby had dismounted his horse to respectfully enter through this same gate in 1918 on foot, apparently as awestruck by this city as Ben was every time he entered it. Ben turned right once he was past David's Tower and headed in the direction of the Armenian Quarter, but before he reached the Christ Church he turned left between it and the church bookstore onto Maronite Convent Street and headed up a very narrow passageway. It was little more than an alley and he followed it up a slight incline and left around a slow arc past the brightly coloured metal doors of peoples' homes built into the stone and cement remnants of Turkish Ottoman and even Crusader-aged buildings. He found the small identifying sign above the gated door of the Maronite Convent and rang the bell. He had made some enquiries a few days earlier as to room availability. He wanted to stay a month, to eat and sleep and work from there. He had not received an answer to his enquiries as to whether a room was available, but now he would find out.

He already knew that the Maronites were a Lebanese Eastern Catholic religious group with claims back to apostolic succession, that they were originally followers of a fifth century monk named Maroun. This convent whose doorbell he was ringing housed a small community of Maronite nuns, all of them but one from Lebanon, who had lived most of their lives here in Jerusalem holding and protecting some sacred space in the Holy City for their particular faith tradition. They lived a quiet, simple life, conducting prayer services and running their hostel for pilgrims as a way of funding their own meagre existence. Grateful to find he was able and welcome to stay, Ben found the gentle nuns to be kind and friendly, and predictably sheltered. At breakfast and teatime which he shared with them each morning and evening, they asked many questions about his experiences in this their city — a city that they lived in but knew almost nothing of. They lived their sheltered lives behind the cloistered walls of the convent leaving its confines only if necessary, bothering no one and being bothered not at all by anyone else either. The Israeli-Arab tensions that lived with great intensity in the streets around them and penetrated the very soul of the city almost everywhere seemed not to ever come past the locked metal doors of their refuge. But they were interested in what was happening "out there" if some outsider would only tell them. As the day ended in the alcove off the convent kitchen where he joined the women to peel potatoes or cut beans with them as they prepared for their meals the next day, the sisters plied Ben with questions through the only English speaking nun among them. In turn, he would ask them about their traditions in relationship to the Armenians down the street, or the Roman Catholic Church which they were so close to in belief and practice and yet separate from in that they had their own bishop and liturgy.

Ben was fascinated by the variety of faith expressions he was coming in contact with in this lively religious city, and he soon developed a new routine for alternate mornings as he made his way to a local library to research, to do some writing, or just spend time thinking and discovering.

The routine he followed after a brief breakfast of yogurt, bread and cheese, a boiled egg and coffee with the sisters, and a guest or two who might be staying in the convent hospice as well, was to leave the quiet and serene quarters of the convent. He clanged through the metal door and turning left he headed in an easterly direction away from the Jaffa Gate angling him through the narrow winding lanes of the Old City until he reached the low doorway of Pathros, a tailor.

Pathros was Syrian Orthodox, the *muktar*, or mayor, in fact the head civilian of the small and shrinking Syrian Orthodox community still remaining in the Old City of Jerusalem. Pathros was warm and friendly, wise and philosophical. He always seemed happy to see Ben. He would quickly prepare a cup of thick Turkish coffee, warming the contents of each cup to near boiling with a small electrical heater coil inserted directly in turn, into each of their cups of the thick brown liquid. As they drank the sweet, rich coffee and ate miniature exotic Turkish, Lebanese, or other Arabic sweets left over from yesterday's sales at the bakery around the corner, the two shared stories.

Pathros chronicled the wars that had come and gone over his sixty-something years in Jerusalem, noting that the people of his particular community tried to stay out of the skirmishes as much as they could, hoping to stay safe and tending to make peace with whomever it was in charge at any given moment in time. They hoped, simply, to continue as much as they could with the life and rituals of their own tradition.

"As Arabic speakers it sometimes becomes more difficult when we are living under a non-Arabic jurisdiction," Pathros mused, "but for the most part I have made suits for some of the most important leaders in Jerusalem regardless of their political or religious stripe. It doesn't matter whether you're King Hussein, Mayor Teddy Kolleck or Prime-Minister Menachem Begin, you need quality suits," he would laugh. Then he would become more serious, noting that what he worried most about was that the young people of his Syrian Orthodox community were leaving. "To America, Canada, Australia and Europe, our young people are going," he said. "Even as young people they are tired of the stress, the fight-ing around them, and as our community gets smaller there is less and less of a chance that they can find suitable mates from within our village of people. The young know that the only way to retain their own identity and that of our people is to marry from within. But who is left? Who will they marry? And how from such a small community and gathering can they hope to find a suitable match?"

On Ben's third or fourth visit with the tailor, Pathros seemed to shake himself out of the melancholy caused by a nearly constant reflection upon his people's increasingly dire situation and asked, "And you, Ben, your people? Where are they from? Surely they have not always lived in Canada?" Ben explained that his parents had emigrated to Canada from Russia, from Siberia, in fact, that anarchy and oppres-sion under the communists, and the breaking down of Tsarist rule that had lent some decency to the country, at least for the Mennonites, had sent his grandfathers and grandmoth-ers packing and running off to far away places, not unlike the Jews heading into the Diaspora. Ben wondered why he had introduced the Jews into the conversation but he realized it was not completely accidental. In this oriental milieu, subtle introductions of controversial topics of discussion were an art form, one he was learning. It was always fascinating to see the response it elicited.

"The Jewish existence in every non-Jewish nation is an interesting one," the tailor volunteered speaking with the gravity befitting a community elder as Ben sipped his coffee, "and it remains a wonder to me that they alone get persecuted in every country they are in. All of us other people, we have known persecution and ridicule and hard times, even genocide in various countries, to be sure, you know the Armenian story, but it seems to me the Jews can know they will be in trouble no matter where they live. And yet sometimes I think they...." His voice trailed off. Pathros, the Syrian Orthodox tailor, also knew the politics of not saying too much aloud in this city, so he would not be quoted or questioned for having triangled himself into situations too complicated to disentangle from.

Ben appreciated Pathros. He felt affection and compassion for this kind, gentle and worldly wise man, and harboured a growing interest in him personally; from Pathros he felt the warmth of a grandfather, or an elderly uncle. The conversations the two of them shared were always interesting, always building and empowering. Their shared words and stories extended Ben's search for social, religious and spiritual meaning, they widened his library of impressions of this exotic and complicated city.

Leaving Pathros' warm studio-workshop cave with its Syrian Orthodox iconography, religious paintings and pictures of the tailor with important people hanging on the whitewashed plaster walls between dark suits at various stages of completion on hangers, Ben would wind down and then up and around the steps of the narrow streets and alleys and into the walkways of newer streets of limestone construction, past the ruins of the Hurva Synagogue, also known as the Hurvat Rabbi Yehudah HaChassid Synagogue. This synagogue, which would one day be rebuilt, still showed signs of the 1948 War and was surrounded by wreckage, despite the high arch built to mark the site. Passing through where the shadow of its eventual front door would fall, Ben dropped down into a small square. Here he would shout a greeting to Avraham, an orthodox Jewish bookseller, shopkeeper and storyteller extraordinaire, who grew up in Canada, but now lived fully the life of a hard-wired "back to the land" religious Zionist waiting always to tell a story, recall a biblical prophecy that had been fulfilled in modern Israel, hear a story, preach a sermon, shock a Christian, or create an exchange with anyone interested in things biblical, things religious, things political or controversial, things worth discussing, things Jewish, things of faith. From Avraham, Ben heard of Old Testament prophecies coming to life in present day Jerusalem and *Erez Yisrael*, and of Christians, crazy, many of them, Avraham would say, disgustingly evangelistic, but sympathetic, yes, sympathetic, of Israel and the Jewish people. He heard too of weak-minded, leftwing Israelis who would give everything back to the Palestinians for a feeble promise of peace and again incur the wrath of G-d "…who though faithful Himself cannot abide unfaithfulness in His chosen people."

Ben found Avraham to be a walking, talking encyclopedia of Jewish religious, historical, philosophical and political knowledge with abundant strongly held opinions and passions for endless hours of storytelling and learning. Often he did not get away from Avraham's store and bookshop until nearly noon, though he had left the Maronite Convent just after breakfast between seven and eight. Like his talks with Pathros, Ben's time with Avraham built his spiritual awareness library, stoked his mind with new impressions and hard questions, changed perceptions and hitherto unexplored speculations.

Finally, with the sun high in the sky above the city, its limestone walls already absorbing the heat of the middle-Eastern sun that shone so relentlessly every day from March or April right through to October or November, and sometimes longer, blazing itself into the life of everyone who lived in this city, Ben stepped out of Avraham's shop. He headed south into an alley parallel to the Western (Wailing) Wall, but a half kilometre or so west of what was left of Herod's Wall, and continually a hotbed of discussion and disagreement between the Jews and the Arabs, especially around issues of archaeological diggings and discovery close to and under the Wall. He stopped in front of a sunken Palestinian pita bakery, its floor at least a metre below the level of the cobbled street, to breathe in the delicious aroma of baking bread that passersby could easily connect to that of their best notions of heaven and life itself. Bending down and looking into the scorching shop, Ben would catch the attention of the Palestinian baker as he inserted or removed freshly made pitas from a large open-ended oven with a long wooden paddle at the other end of the cave-like bakery. When he was free from his immediate tasks, the baker with sweat beaded on his forehead, his shirt soaked, would pass up the special pita he had set aside for Ben, whom he knew would come looking for at about this time. The baker and Ben had never had a conversation for they shared no common language, but an intimate connection around giving and receiving bread had been built between these two strangers. They wordlessly respected one another, it seemed, though they shared literally no knowledge of one another other than their smiles and a willingness for Ben to pay and the baker to give for free, all nurtured by Ben taking the time to often stand and appreciatively watch the artist baker making and baking his fare. Somehow Ben came to know that the baker and his family were Palestinian, and he knew they were Muslim. The baker probably assumed Ben was an American, and possibly not Jewish. Clearly, though, in their many encounters the baker handing Ben his warm pita in a green, waxy, opaque bag, and Ben bowing and saying "*Shukran*" they became brothers of a kind. Brothers who connected over something very small that felt deep.

No wonder Jesus called himself the *Bread of Life* in this place and instituted his memorial supper around bread such as this, Ben thought one day, clutching his precious pita. On this particular day the baker had upped the ante of the contents of the green bag he had ready for Ben by adding two boiled eggs, still warm, and a paper twist of hyssop to dip the bread in for an added flavour of heaven. Ben could only smile as he anticipated eating it as he walked or sitting on a limestone boulder overlooking the startling green beauty of the Hinnom valley just minutes away. Some days Ben would attempt to pay the baker double the standard fare for pita in the market before he stepped away from the bakery entrance, and sometimes it was received.

To Ben the relationship around this bread was about giving and receiving. That was clear. The baker knew well the art of generous living: an exchange of affection and dignity. It was never pure when it went only one way. And in Jerusalem bread was special, more than flour and water, yeast and salt. It carried brotherhood and spirituality, deep connections beyond words; it pointed to life and relationship. It had been said that a loaf of bread was made up of the crumbs of the sacred. It shocked Ben whenever he saw a piece of pita discarded on the narrow street edges, or left over on a dirty plate after a meal. He almost felt as if he had come upon a broken body left unburied in a war zone, or an accident victim unattended beside a car wreck.

From the baker's step Ben turned toward the bullet-pocked Zion's Gate leading out onto Mt. Zion with its David's Tomb, Upper Room, Armenian Church, Muslim Minaret, graveyards, including a rare Protestant cemetery overlooking the Hinnom Valley, and the high wall that marked the southern edge of old Jerusalem ever since the Turkish architect builder of the Wall had left Mount Zion outside its safety zone, an oversight for which he reportedly lost his head. Just inside Zion Gate, however, Ben stopped to chat with the Armenian shopkeepers struggling to keep themselves alive in what once was a vibrant Armenian Quarter and a place of extraordinary business. Over glasses of cold water or dark tea with floating peppermint leaves the conversations nearly always went to differences of faith and religion, and the profound questions of how much one could mix them all together and not get lost. Or found.

Ben relished these days of exchange and discovery, the conversations about life from perspectives and experiences radically different from his own. The words exchanged, especially those specific to the faith of the storytellers, often told with the passion of an enflamed evangelist, sharpened Ben's understanding of his own faith and heritage, his own history, identity and culture of belief, and he was enriched.

Chapter 12
Blyumshteyn, The Ukraine — 1876

The power of the Tsarist system was beginning to show cracks. Intellectuals, artists, anarchists and idealists of a myriad of sorts conceived of a new day for Mother Russia, revolutionary ideas abounded and plots to assassinate Tsar Alexander II were rumoured and real. The rule of law was eroding and criminal acts visited against minorities were less and less punished, less and less reported. There was no use in appealing to the authorities; if they cared they had no means by which to bring any power to bear on those flouting the law anyway. Anti-Semitism in all its forms continued to thrive and even increased. Anarchy ruled. The once great Holy Russia from its magnificently cultured cities in the west to its far-flung peasant villages further east seemed to be declining and drifting toward ruin.

It was late fall, one of those years where two disparate calendars were going to place Chanukah and Christmas close together. Away from the cities which celebration one participated in depended on what village one looked at life from. Grigory, a Jewish subsistence farmer, as were most farmers in this part of the world, wandering tailor and "hired man" of the local estate owner had finally returned to his home and family from his late fall trek through the shadowy Jewish *shtetls* and the more visible Mennonite villages in the region. He arrived at his home in Blyumshteyn just in time to be present as Rivka gave birth to twin girls. The birth of any child is the most profound fist that one can raise against hopelessness; twins is a double fist. Grigory and Rivka's spirits rose.

The local brigands skulking about in these parts of the Ukraine, known as Molotschna to the majority Mennonites and others in the area, had helped themselves on numerous occasions to Grigory's grain, livestock, food stores, homemade wine, and bolts of cloth, which they just threw in the mud, but now, as impossible as it seemed, they were becoming even more desperate, more depraved than ever. Grigory knew that the next time they rode into his settlement he would have to do something to defend his small family for there was nothing left to appease these monsters who allowed themselves to visit any horror they could think of upon any victims they could find.

Winter had come early by the time the family was able to celebrate that the twins were three months old and on a day that should have carried some anticipated hope for the coming Chanukah celebrations in Grigory and Rivka's community, the word went out that the horrible horsemen were heading their way again. The sun was going down on a night that was sure to be cold to add to the misery that so much early snow had brought. Grigory and Rivka had discussed what they might do when the desperados came again. They had heard that these men were actually killing some of their victims now, and the villagers had become afraid for their children, and afraid for the very survival of their tiny community as a whole. Their Jewish forefathers had known persecution in virtually every place they had lived; their Ukrainian sojourn was not turning out to be any friendlier.

The older boys of Blyumshteyn, who in summer often served as sheep and cattle herders for the Mennonite landowners and for those few Jewish villagers who had been able to procure some animals, were stationed in the woodlots at the edge of their haphazard settlement during these days of rumours, to watch and warn the settlers should the horses and their usually drunken riders come their way. Then the warning came. A dozen or more horsemen were on the other side of the nearest woodlot armed with rifles and burning torches, and it sounded like they were arguing about which way to go, which group of villages to "pick" this night.

Grigory nodded to Rivka when the word came that the bandits were on the move and coming their way. Tearfully but with deft hands Rivka fetched and readied the small wicker basket fitted with blankets and soft cloths. Her mind ran to a famous wicker basket escape in her people's history; she could only pray for some kind of a similar outcome. Grigory bundled himself up in his warmest coat and pulled on his high, horsehair lined winter boots. The couple made no eye contact, made no conversation. Their sorrow was beyond words. They moved with resolve.

With the basket readied, Rivka quickly wrapped the twin they had agreed on, the one who seemed slightly stronger than the other, the more demanding and aggressive of the two, in a patchwork quilt of bright blues and reds handed down from a previous generation for firstborns in her family. Somehow the journey Rivka was about to send her child on warranted a first-born blessing regardless of birth order. Rivka tied two leather laces around both ends of a blanket wrapped around the fidgety child, not so tightly that the bundle would be airtight, but tightly enough to keep the baby warm. It was at least two *verst* through the woods and across the fields to where Grigory was taking the child, and the weather was fiercely cold

"Do you remember where you're taking the baby?" she asked. Neither she nor Grigory noticed that they had not used the child's name again since they made the decision to do what they were now doing. They did not know they were

DANNY UNRAU

trying to separate themselves from her to ease the horrible pain of what was transpiring. "Who you're giving her to?" Rivka whispered, hoping, praying, that they would get their plan deployed before the dreaded horses could be heard in the walkway outside their home above the inevitable shouting and the swearing of the terrible men that would transpire if they came. Yet as much as she knew she must do what she was doing, she was filled with guilt and an enormous sense of maternal inadequacy for what she and her husband were about to execute.

"Yes, of course! To a Mr. David Ratzlaff and his wife in Blumenstein, the Mennonite village. I told you. I sew their clothes and they're always kind. They're trustworthy. They'll look after our baby, keep her alive. It is nearly their high holiday of giving and getting gifts and God will guide them, I'm sure. Though I don't know that they will raise her as we would. But it is our duty to see that we keep one of us alive," he panted between sentences as he pulled on his boots.

"I thought it was a Mr. Peter and his wife?" Rivka hissed, as if the approaching riders could hear her.

"No, I told you. A Mr. David and his wife," Grigory stammered, registering annoyance at her, but at his core outraged that there was so much wrong with their world and the horror that they had to take such measures to keep their own God-given child alive.

"It doesn't matter whom, Grigory, or how they raise her," Rivka sobbed, wanting to believe it herself, "as long as she will be able to live." The grieving couple stood looking at one another now; their pain riveting them together as their lives felt torn apart. "Are we choosing the right thing, Grigory? Are we doing the right thing?" Rivka cried.

Someone ran down the narrow path past their place shouting, "The men are close! And they are carrying fire. The men are coming close! They are also crazy drunk." Grigory pulled a scarf up over his nose toward the lower rim of his fur hat. Rivka kissed the squirming bundle now in the basket and with tears coursing her cheeks pushed her husband and his precious bundle out the back door of their tiny home. She could see her husband kick open the gate in the picket fence half covered with snow and disappear into the dark around the corner of the blacksmith shop and the store behind their house.

Rivka sat down on the floor, cupped her hands in her face, and wept. The other twin, Sophia, stirred in her rocking cradle; Rivka could have moved the cradle with her foot to sooth the child, but she picked the baby up and opening her blouse, nursed her, more for herself than for the child. Still wondering, still weeping, still not knowing whether they were doing the right thing. For the rest of her life the question would nag her; she would die without knowing the answer.

Grigory ploughed through the snow that was up to his knees, struggled through a bluff of poplar trees where the snow was even deeper than it had been in the village and started across the open fields. The night was moonlit and clear enough that he could see where he was going, and still pushing through the deep fresh snow his mind asked the questions not unlike the ones Rivka was asking at home. His bundle was not overly heavy, not physically, anyway, but it seemed the heaviest thing he had ever carried. Grigory wondered if he would ever see this child again. The little girl had obviously fallen asleep for she made no sound. After an hour or so of pressing through the snow and keeping an eye open to make sure he was not being followed, Grigory could finally see the dim lights of the Mennonite village that was his goal. He prayed that God, blessed be He, would see to it that the people he thought kind were kind indeed.

As he approached the edge of the village and gained its edges, he thought he saw the moving shadows of boys between trees, around buildings; these people, too, were watching for the unpredictable marauders. Grigory knew this village well, and he hurried down the trodden snow path between the rows of housebarns. These Mennonite villages were different than his own settlement, in some very different ways — less haphazard, less thrown-together, more organized, more permanent, more established.

He shifted his bundle from one arm to the other, wished he could stop and open it and see his daughter one more time. But there was no time; he must not be seen. He wondered if the youthful sentinels in the shadows were following him or if they had stayed at the village boundary, and then concluded they would not be afraid of a lone Jew running down their main street with a package.

Grigory stopped for a second at the gate of another family he knew well, whose large house meant they were wealthier than the Ratzlaffs, but then kept going. The smell of fresh food, bread and salt ham, fried potatoes & *grüben smaltz* along with the odour of sweet manure coursed past the edges of his hat and scarf, still pulled up to just below his eyes, and up into his nose. He looked for the light of a lantern or a Christmas candle, any light, through the shuttered front windows of the home he was looking for that would indicate someone was in the front room of the house. The room where he had sewn their Sunday clothes.

Grigory puffed up to the front door of the chosen house. He could not take the time to think again about chosenness. His heart was beating fast. Tears frozen on his scarf clouded his vision; tiny icicles of frost hung down from his eyebrows and stuck to his eyelashes. He put the basket down on the front step of the chosen house and family, placing his hand on the still blanket, he uttered a quick firstborn blessing in Hebrew and Yiddish, asked the Lord for forgiveness for himself and protection for this child, then struck the door hard with a mittened fist. Twice. Choking back a huge sob, he ran back through the gate and ducked down behind the picket fence. He peered through the spaces between the fence slats to watch the front door.

In seconds the door opened. David, Grigory's chosen and hopefully righteous Gentile friend, peered out, anxiously; he, too, had known the horror of the brigands, though he had not heard anything this night. Narrowing his eyes to see into the dark, David heard a squeak at his feet, and looking down, saw the basket. He picked it up with both hands, as if lifting baby Moses out of the reeds, and with a booted foot pushed the door shut as he backed into the house.

Grigory wanted to fall face down in the snow and scream or die, or at least cry. Instead, he heaved himself to his feet and turned back the way he had come without looking round. Barely seeing where he was going, his fears turned now toward what he might find when he got home.

"Frieda! Frieda!" David Ratzlaff shouted. "Look at what's been left at our door!" His wife, Elfrieda, came quickly, a baby girl in her arms and a tousled-haired toddler of two or so, a boy, half clinging to her skirt but reaching around for some toy he had dropped as he stumbled along then sensing that something extraordinary was underway. He straightened and quietened.

"What is it?" Elfrieda exclaimed. "It's not quite Christmas yet, and it doesn't look like food. What is it?"

David answered that it could not be food as it made noises. He began to untie the leather laces wrapped around the ends of the blanket bundle. David and Elfrieda would tell each other years later that they knew immediately what that package was that night, but that they had been emotionally unable to absorb the reality as quickly as it was happening, and had opened the mystery package with curiosity.

DANNY UNRAU

"Here," said Elfrieda impatiently, both excitedly and fearfully, handing David the child in her arms. She untied the last lace and unrolled the blanket. Within the layers of cloths appeared the dark wide eyes of a beautiful baby.

"Baby! Baby!" shouted the toddler from between the knees of his parents, in the Low German that some would have said sounded like Yiddish.

"Whose child is this? What is this surprise? Is this a gift from God?" asked Elfrieda, scooping up the child. "Is this a stolen child? Is this ours to keep and care for? Who brought her to us?"

"I think we've been chosen, Frieda," David said, barely above a whisper, "to save a child."

"But a baby changes everything," said Elfrieda, opening the blanket layers further. A note fell out of the folds of the quilted patchwork of blues and reds.

"It does! It does! It will!" David answered. "A baby changes everything."

"Here's a note," cried Elfrieda, as she unfolded it, her hand shaking with excitement. "Can you read it without your glasses, David? I'm not sure what language it's written in, and the letters are very faint."

David reached for the slip of paper and squinting, he said, "It's German and Russian, and I think maybe something else, maybe Yiddish, I don't know. Let me see if I can make out what it says." After a silent few seconds he read:

'Dear friend David, many times I have thought you to be almost like a brother to me as you asked me to sew for you, and as you welcomed me into your home. Many times you have been kind. If you have ever felt, too, a little like a brother to me now I must ask you to be one again. This is my daughter. Save her. I fear we will not survive. I cannot tell you my name. I know you will know who I am, but it must not be known. For my sake, for your sake, for the child's sake. 'Hear O Israel, our God is One,

and we are to love Him and our neighbour' remember David? We have that in common. Remember! Her name is Anna. She has a twin sister named Sophia."

"I cannot say whose child this is, Elfrieda. Its better that you don't know," David stammered, his mind trying to get around the possibilities of what this new reality all meant. "Then you will never have to tell. Her name is Anna Ratzlaff now. She is ours. She will need a special blessing, a love from us as if she were our very own child. A full sister of these two we have already been given by God."

Chapter 13
Dachau, Germany — 1939

Walter Becker was becoming increasingly revolted by the creatures Dachau was creating with its killing culture, but at the same time, he began to sense a growing compassion within his soul for these beings, the first-line victims of this hell. More than likely the two emotions were related. He was not self-aware enough to know whether it was their physical condition, their gross emaciation, or their dead eyes that were invading his spirit. The spiritual and mental breakdown he observed in the inmates, parallel, really, to the spiritual breakdown the German practitioners and creators of this hell were now themselves unconsciously succumbing to even as their victims did, filled him with a revulsion that was becoming more and more difficult to withstand. Just as unconsciously, and not unlike the women of the *Scheisskommando* he was in charge of, Walter wanted to live. The concentration camp, he told his mother while on leave one day, killed everyone, uniformed or un-uniformed, one way or another. Whoever came into Dachau's orb and fell under its killing spell was doomed.

Walter's growing awareness of the hopelessness breeding in the camp sank deep into his spirit. There seemed to be no way to protect oneself no matter who one was. He did not recall that the preachers he grew up under, shouting about hell in their stern sermons, had ever said that one could enter hell even before one dies. Now he knew. The sight and smell of the inmates was grotesque to him, but no less than the sight and smell of the clean and well-fed administrators of the system, he began to notice. He realized that he was at risk of being devoured by this place. He could not know, not yet, that the compassion in his soul that had been nurtured in him by his kind mother as a young boy and fostered by a gentle sense of peoplehood in his tiny childhood faith community was somehow being awakened in this demonic domain. Somewhere in his future, he sensed, if he survived, he would have to do some deep reflection around compassion and righteousness and forgiveness, and around a faith that needed reviving. Without faith, there would be no hope. All these things he began to discern as a guard in the unlikely place called Dachau.

And it had begun — this rebirth, or discovery of spiritual depth, if one could call it that — with Sophia, the woman who became Walter's designated leader of the *Scheisskommando*. He had noticed her almost immediately upon her arrival in Dachau. The dignity she bore, the air with which she walked and talked despite the conditions she had been thrust into in the camp made her an instant leader. She was the kind of person who seemed to be able to retain her self in spite of all odds and circumstances against her. Now Walter did not see her as a woman; he had blanked out the femininity, in fact, the humanity of his charges a long time ago as an unconscious self-protection against feeling anything. But Sophia's strength, her ability to keep on, despite being incessantly degraded by her work, and the poise with which she carried herself even as a *Scheisskommando* member was extraordinary. Walter noticed that she was the only one in the camp who looked him in the eye when he spoke to her. He soon knew that she treated her Jewish companions like they were still what they had been before these days of terror, and he had noticed that she sought to hold them to some semblance of their traditional faith by leading daily prayers and in some form celebrating the Jewish High Holidays, even though she seemed not to be overly religious herself. When Sophia had the opportunities to be alone with her companions and could have conversations with them, she organized the sharing of precious food scraps, secret bits of paper for the writing of notes to family members to be smuggled out of the camp, and she told them often that they were made in the image of God. Sophia was a woman of a formidable force in personality and character.

As Walter had to relate to Sophia by virtue of her assigned leadership with the camp inmates, he gradually came to somewhat know her. At least as much as a guard in a place such as Dachau could know a prisoner. He realized after a few meetings with her that he had to muster his own confidence to prevent feeling inferior to Sophia as he barked out his orders, as he delegated the sanitary work assignments to the women of the *Scheisskommando* every morning after roll call. Everything in his training, everything that the propaganda machine had drilled into his being screamed that he needed to wipe his heart and soul clear of any feelings of respect for these captives. But it was not Sophia who was really getting to him, he cared nothing for these cattle, he told himself, she was just a bony old woman, a Jewess no less, and yet he was drawn by her indomitable bearing, her irrepressible, unmistakable dignity calling to his. He could not know yet that the spirit of truth captured in the Psalmist's description of *deep calls to deep* was breathing life into his soul.

Sophia's personal strength should have gotten her quickly exterminated. Dachau was no place for someone who exuded so much life, but her physical strength gave her value as a worker and kept her from being assigned to the infirmary, or worse, where the women her age usually were sent. Her ability to work also exempted her from being volunteered for the medical experiments Dachau became famous for. Maybe at first she believed the lie *Arbeit Macht Frei* emblazoned over the camp's main gate and perhaps for a time she thought she might be able to earn her freedom. It was, however, her compassion for her campmates that gained her profound influence with them, and for some years saved her life in that it was her leadership amongst her companions, it was argued in the guardroom, that made her a potentially valuable tool for the guards. In actual fact, the guards who worked most closely with her were themselves captured by her, intrigued at her strength of character, though not one of them would ever admit such was the case. Nevertheless, those in control of the women in blocks seventeen and eighteen of the thirty-one barracks at Dachau chose to let her live.

Sophia came to lead the *Scheisskommando* under Walter's command and he more and more gave her snippets of freedom within the horror of the concentration camp culture. This he did by allowing her to accompany the crew that was allowed outside the walls of Dachau to dump the human waste of the camp.

He knew that two things were possible outside the wall: she could escape, or she could connect with the world that lurked there. Everyone knew that there was a clandestine society, even a mini-economy in the woods, relating to the people who came and went in its shadows, and that these women carried the currency of that world across the line between the two.

Could it be that Sophia was somehow chosen to be a kind of light for the people of Dachau who came in contact with her? Are there people who get that call? Surely many of them, at least the female prisoners in her bunk, carried a collective understanding of persecution that all their people had known for millennia, but what made her different? How was it that she was affecting her captors? And how was it that her spirit was burrowing its way even into the souls of her captors, and especially Walter's? It might have been his noticing that even with the restraints placed upon her she maintained a spiritual centre tied to her religious tradition of righteousness. Somehow he as a free guard had not had the courage or the drive to maintain even a strong connection to his own spiritual heritage. It began to occur to Walter, however, that it was the inherent spirituality of Sophia's faith tradition that gave her the ability to remain a person, a *mensch,* in spite of everything. Most of her people, however, he argued with himself, had not been able to maintain themselves body and soul in Dachau as she had, but it seemed that Sophia's wholeness was not just that she was a remarkable individual, her wholeness was clearly a blending and a coming together of her personality, her personal history, her people, and her rich heritage. Sophia was the sum total of far more than just herself.

As time passed Walter realized he was being drawn by a power larger than himself and against which he had no inner muscle to withstand. He sensed this energy drawing him related entirely to his own identity and being and a need to discover it. By the time he was hearing that the war might turn against Germany, and change, which at one time had seemed so impossible in what had been so monstrously and powerfully created by the Nazis, was in the air, he realized he needed to be careful around his awe for what Sophia reflected and represented. Dachau was a poison. And death. For all. That much he now knew. What Sophia brought to her world seemed like life. How could he integrate such opposites in this place, in his life?

Chapter 14
Jerusalem, Israel — 2000

It was just past midnight and Ben Ruhe was on the late bus to Jerusalem after having seen his latest tour group to Israel off at the Ben Gurion airport. He had prearranged a room in the Montifiori Hotel just a few steps from the corner of Ben Yehuda and King George Streets, and in spite of his excitement managed to be asleep by two a.m. The next day he took some rooms on Tchernikovsky Street and quickly organized his lodgings so that he would be as free as possible to engage in what was most important — daily sorties into the dynamic streets of Jerusalem for stories and conversations.

In the years since Ben had last been in the Golden City a vibrant coffee café culture had arisen and he soon knew most of the locations of the *Aroma* coffee bars around the city. One could never find a deserted *Aroma* bar; more often than not the tables and chairs were fully occupied. When he could find a vacant space in one of these bars, Ben would order a typical Israeli breakfast which included a finely chopped salad of tomatoes, green onions and cucumbers, scrambled eggs, Bulgarian cheese, a thick slice of fresh brown bread and a steaming cappuccino, log onto the internet on his laptop, and, then, invariably losing interest in it, would get into conversation with the people at the tables around him. Holocaust survivors, Israeli Arab construction workers, retirees suffering from Post-traumatic stress disorder, *kibbutzniks*, Yeshiva students, university grads, tourists, cabdrivers, journalists, young moms, soldiers, waiters from other restaurants, Americans, Germans, Swedes, Aussies, and every other kind of person who found some reason to be in Jerusalem, populated the busy coffee bars. There was never any shortage of people with whom one could have a fascinating conversation, despite the fact that most were at first surprised to be engaged by a total stranger.

One morning, cramped in a hoped-for quiet corner in the *Aroma* on Emek Refaim Street, and despite having really wanted to get some writing finished, Ben struck up a conversation with a thirty-something former Yeshiva student named Doron, who could not seem to make up his mind whether he was a religious Jew or not. Until he encountered a Gentile Christian. Then simply being in the presence of a Gentile of the Jesus persuasion fostered in him a sudden, near vicious passion for his own faith. At such times he became a zealot, in attitude almost reminiscent of the *Sicarri* of two thousand years ago who carried knives to deftly and fatally make their passionate religio-political points in these same streets.

Ben and Doron very quickly entered into an intense but mostly respectful conversation, their coffees and breakfasts quickly forgotten. Doron assailed Ben with familiar horror stories of Christian religious and social arrogance; Ben responded with clarifying questions and stories of his own of positive living in Israel, about the *kibbutzim* he knew, prevalent Israeli attitudes, and sprinkled in some of his own knowledge of Judaism itself.

"For a Gentile, a Christian, you seem to know a lot about Jews and Judaism, and I am intrigued that you have so much interest in Israel," opined a coffee drinker at the next table, who had unapologetically been listening in on the exchange and obviously wanted to be part of the repartee.

"And you must admit that Christianity has nothing to do with Judaism," Doron fired into the air, choosing to ignore the man trying to barge into the conversation.

"It has everything to do with Judaism. It came directly out of Judaism. Its founder, Jesus or Jeshuah, as some prefer to call him, was a practicing Orthodox Jew, and Christianity's first commentator, Paul, was a learned Pharisee, a student of Gamaliel, the grandson of Hillel. What do you mean Christianity has nothing to do with Judaism?"

"That's crap," shouted Doron, "and you know it. First, your Jesus and then your apostle Paul, if they didn't completely reject all Jewish tradition around the breaking of the Sabbath and the Kosher food laws, certainly took great pains at times to distance themselves from proper practice. I would suggest you're seriously reconstructing history to say what you say. I have reasons to believe that history proves that Christianity and Judaism are diametrically opposed, and most of the people in this room would agree!" He waved his arms sweeping all the patrons of the coffee shop into a symbolic single unit.

"The whole world has often agreed on something totally wrong," Ben countered, "you should well know that, nevertheless, our two faiths are not opposed, as you say. In fact, I'd say it's unfortunate that we have come to talk about Christianity and Judaism as two faiths, rather than a variant on one. I would submit that they shared something absolutely remarkable right at the outset, to be positive, and what's more, to be negative, both present-day orthodox Judaism and orthodox Christianity are sorry shadows of their intended selves. That much they have in common." Ben looked around to see what the audience was doing with his speech.

The room seemed to have frozen. For a brief moment those listening were silent before some moved to respond.

Doron, however, was the first to respond. "I'm offended! I don't appreciate the little word trick you just played here." But he was clearly not yet finished with this conversation. His upbringing, education and situation in life made him well suited for disagreement. He and most of his café mates were the same in that regard. Disagreement in the streets of Jerusalem among people still willing to talk almost never caused the ending of relationships, nor did disagreements usually end conversations. They simply raised the level of exchange. Ben had to fight off some of his ingrained Canadian tendencies to politeness to keep the conversation going from his end. Knowing that he was clearly the lone Gentile in this room, and as essentially safe that might be in actuality, his national tendency tugged at his emotions to restrain himself a little. But he had been in Israel too many times, absorbed the natural confidence and the inherent assertiveness of the people of this land to politely back off, plus he was by this time far too invested in this conversation to retreat.

"Well I'm more than offended by our history, I'm ashamed and outraged," Ben continued, "and you have every right to be offended, and more, by the history of Christian treatment of your people, Doron, but you need not be offended by the parallels and the commonness of Christianity and Judaism. In fact, I think a Christianity that wants to tip its hat to Judaism could be seen as a positive. Such is showing respect and gratitude. I could truthfully say that what's best and pure in Christianity is all from Judaism, and things Jewish. Period! And I believe that completely."

"Well, I need more," the other man said, making a gesture of frustration. "You must tell me, my friend, what on earth's the same, what's different that brings you to your insulting position of our commonness. I can't get past the emotion of a horrible history between us, and the church's role in anti-Semitism. How can you ignore that?"

The gentleman at the next table wanting to be an interloper interjected with a loud "Whoa!" grinning wolfishly as if what had just been said made delicious points for him as he looked around the room for assenting allies. One of the *Aroma* staff members brought Ben and Doron refills of their coffees, but they, too, would grow cold unfinished.

"I can't ignore our terrible history," Ben went on, "and my apologies must sound trite, but I think it was one of your rabbis who said, 'While it is not mine to complete the task, neither am I allowed to refrain from attempting to do so.' I acknowledge our sin, and I use the word, sin, deliberately, to describe our too often horrific institutional and individual treatment of the Jewish people. We were wrong; none of what we did in the name of Jesus that was anti-Semitic lines up with what Jesus really taught and modelled."

"But that's just *your* opinion," countered Doron. "You have more than a few million Christians to convince of your position. Maybe you should stop trying to save the Jews in all your proselytizing and clean up your house."

"Our house needs cleaning. There can be no doubt about that," Ben conceded. "But to the question: what's the same, what's different in our faiths that could lead us to peaceful coexistence? I think three things."

"I'd say a lot more than just three things, how about six million?" interjected the cheerleader from the next table, who with the encouraging murmurs of agreement, cheers and nods to his input by his coffee shop neighbours had by now pulled his chair up to the table Ben and Doron were sitting at. Doron glanced at the invader, but seemed not to see him.

"The value of the lives of my grandparents who died in Auschwitz rest on your argument," Doron ventured. To Ben, Doron's words sounded like a threat, like all of history between their people suddenly depended on his words.

"Your grandparents lives were of inestimable value, Doron, by virtue of who they were as human beings, by who created them 'Blessed be he!' My words don't add to their worth, but let me give you my three points? For starters, Judaism is interested in people doing the will of God, and Christianity is interested in salvation, redemption, being made new, in essence being made righteous in believing in and following Christ, and that implies finding God's will. The two are not that far apart. Secondly, and already implied in the first point, what Judaism seeks is to bring the world a stage nearer to righteousness, and Christianity seeks to bring people to Christ, for the ultimate same-wished-for result, relational, daily, spiritual righteousness. Thirdly, the Jews are by definition a people, a natural community, and Christians in authentically following the rabbi Jesus are made into a people, a gathered community, as well, and as this new people adheres to Christ's ethic, it is righteous, righteous in ways already defined by the Jewish faith, as it is pure."

Ben kept talking, "I don't believe Jesus came to start a new religion. I think he was inherently non-religious in the current use of the language. In North America, at least, religion is a bad word. Jesus came to foster a relationship with people to in turn foster a freely chosen relationship between God and humans. It's not so un-Jewish to want a dynamic, living, relationship with God, is it? In fact, I think what Jesus would have wanted, and I add, wants now, is a combination of what was meant and intended in Judaism and in Christianity at their respective purest best. That's all. Jesus was above labels and handles. And if I could add something more that would indicate how closely we are tied, I'd say your covenant is from Moses, mine is from Noah. These two covenants, different in degree and number only, wouldn't you say?

"You're killing me here," Doron grinned crookedly, "with your talk of a pure combination of Judaism and Christianity.

After all that's happened, that can't happen. There is no pure left. Not for me, not for anyone I know, neither in your world nor mine."

"I'm sorry," said Ben, "I am sorry. About so much. With your rabbis who said that we essentially kill when we cause the blood to drain from someone's face, I don't want to drain the blood from your face. I don't want to kill you. I would want to call you my brother, and I don't want to risk offending your sensibilities. I have not, and we Christians have not yet earned the right to even affectionate name-calling. I pray for the day."

The café fell silent. It was as if it was suddenly compressed with too much feeling. Ben and Doron both, for the first time in a half hour or so, took sips of their cold coffee. They looked at each other and said nothing more. Whether either one of them or both shrugged as a way to punctuate the end of their conversation no one in the coffee shop would have noticed as everyone suddenly looked to their own cups for hot coffee, or the Jerusalem Post and other headlines, all at once demanded attention.

Chapter 15
The Ukraine, Crimea, Siberia, Germany – 1876–1896

The Ratzlaff family did not say anything in their community about how they suddenly had a new baby that appeared to be around three months of age. The elders and the women of the village suspected the truth, but said nothing. The children began to wonder if there was something about the birds and the bees and the arrival of children that they had not yet learned from the most earthy and colourful children of their friendship circle, which to varying degrees included all the kids of the village. The older teenage girls said it was obvious some relative had gotten pregnant out of wedlock "back home," probably in Chortiza, or some such place, and the unwed mother's family had to wait for the child to be big enough to travel before they had it brought to relatives where it would not be an embarrassment. Despite great potential for misinformation, there really were not many secrets in a village of this size, and in this Mennonite culture, where gossip was not as roundly criticized and preached against as was dancing, drinking Vodka, playing sporting games on Sundays, and appearing in public in such a way as to embarrass one's parents, the church, and the Mennonites as a whole.

Gradually people forgot that Anna seemed not to have come into the Ratzlaff family in the usual way, and with skin and eye colour not so extraordinary, she blended in. Anna was never told where she came from either. She thought she had arrived just like her siblings. She had no reason to think otherwise. The relative ages of the Ratzlaff children, despite the closeness in age between Anna and her little sister were all within the range of biological possibility, and there was, therefore, no cause for alarm or wonder. How could Anna not think that she was just another Mennonite girl growing up in a Mennonite village in the places she lived growing up from the Molotschna to Crimea to Neu Samara and finally Siberia before leaving Russia altogether?

The family left Blumstein when Anna was six and she happily began her education in the Crimean Mennonite village of Spat. She loved school and worked hard at her lessons, helped her mother as did all the girls of the village, and David and Elfrieda Ratzlaff, in their unabated love for this girl left on their doorstep, gave her absolutely no reason to suspect she had not been born to them. Anna listened no more intently than the other children to the stories about the differences between Russians and Mennonites, Jews and Mennonites, all others and Mennonites. By age ten Anna thought she heard in her father, David, a more positive tone toward the Jewish villagers who used to live down the road than what she heard from her friends, her teachers and in church, and she even said so one day, causing David's heart to skip a beat. Anna's arrival in his family was a secret he was determined to keep, regardless of the potential cost for harboring such important identifying information.

David told his children at the supper table one day that the Jewish villages some miles from their home had been burnt out by bandits, and that all the Jewish people of the community had either been killed or had somehow escaped. He commented that he hoped many of those Jewish people he had come to know had survived, and if they had, he wondered, too, where they were now. More he never said.

He would never know that Grigory and Rivka and their little Sophia, Anna's twin, had survived. They had escaped their burning home torched by brigands and looters in Blyumshteyn one horrific night not long after Grigory had left Anna at Ratzlaff's door and, even more miraculously, had safely walked miles and months before finally finding themselves in Germany. They survived the ravages of World War I but Rivka died soon thereafter. Grigory lived to be a rather elderly man and died without experiencing the full horror of Nazi Germany, but his daughter was the remarkable woman Jewish woman named Sophia remembered by both surviving inmates, and even some of the guards, as having been a prisoner in Dachau after the war ended. She was unforgettable to many.

Anna, growing up like her Mennonite siblings and friends, was singularly sensitive in her spirit toward God. By age eight she had begun to ask her mother if she could be baptized. Only once did David and his wife, Elfrieda, glance at one other sharply when Anna asked at the table, again, whether they thought the church elders would consider her for baptism at her age, as if it seemed she thought she would not be eligible for one reason or another. David never talked to his wife about the interesting struggle in his spirit about Anna being baptized. He sensed a conflict in his loyalty between his faith in Jesus and the Great Commission that compelled them to lead all to be disciples of Christ, not the least of which should be his children, and to the Jewish man who had placed this child in his care to be saved. "Well," David thought, "Anna is being saved, and I should be happy." But he was still uneasy around Anna's talk of Christian baptism, and that in itself was sobering, and even guilt inducing in his own Mennonite spirit and soul. With Grigory so long ago gone, and possibly not even alive anymore, he had no one now to talk with about the dynamic between the two particular faiths and peculiar peoples.

In the end, Anna parents, David and Elfrieda, suggested that she pray, listen carefully to God's voice and her teachers, and read her Bible. The Lord would prepare a time and a way for her to be baptized, they told her. The young girl was happy, despite the occasional childhood worries fanned by the increasing conversation in their home and village that the world was changing, and endured the long trek north and east the family made moving with other landless Mennonite families from Spat in the Crimea to Neu Samara in eastern European Russia, and then all the way to Siberia.

Anna was seventeen by time the family settled in Neu Samara and connecting with a group of young people from the newly formed Mennonite Brethren Church she approached the leaders of her family's new church community to be baptized. Not long thereafter the baptism took place in the river not far from the village in a quiet corner of the woods. As the newly baptized ones gathered after the service to be individually blessed and congratulated on their decision to be followers of Jesus, David handed his daughter a card on the back of which he had painstakingly printed, from his Bible, words from 1 Peter 2:9, with his own one word addition in brackets: *But you are (from) a chosen people, a royal priesthood, a holy nation, a people belonging to God, that you may declare the praises of him who called you out of darkness into his wonderful light.* Anna would never realize the double meaning buried in the Bible verse her father had given her; decades later some of her descendents would catch the hidden reference to her heritage one day and would know exactly what her father was trying to tell her even in the midst of his silence and deep resolve not to break her personal and family secret.

Anna had been baptized with a larger group of young men and women in a quiet curve in the river significantly unknown in the forest to many for the reason that the Mennonites were coming under increasing persecution, even from within the wider Mennonite community, and they hoped that their sacred and celebratory rite would not attract too much attention in any of the communities unlike their own in the region. Being different from the Russian norm, as varied as the society was, was becoming more of a problem, not less, despite the fact that there were winds of change blowing across greater Russia suggesting that some of the old ways of doing things were ending in Russia and unpredictable new ways would follow.

David and Elfrieda did not find settling in New Samara easy or satisfactory and began wondering and praying about moving again. They investigated the possibility of following some of their relatives who had already relocated in Canada. But Anna worried about leaving when she heard her father express his thoughts; she was beginning to have feelings for one of the young men from the group that she had been baptized with, and she thought he liked her, too. He had smiled at her at choir practice one week and had actually stood quite close to her when the group was talking after church a couple of Sundays after that, she remembered, as her father spoke of leaving. The young man, Cornelius, was the youngest son of the Peter Klassens, a musical family, and she did not know whether his family was talking about going to Canada as well or not. She needed to find out.

Anna's mother, Elfrieda, always said that Anna was the most determined and most assertive of her brood of children. She told people, often with a slight touch of pride, that when her Anna wanted something, she usually got it. Elfrieda would watch Anna with a special look sometimes and muse how much she was not her child in some of her unique ways of being. She was strong and single-minded; she carried a dignity and a determination, as if she had a mysterious double portion of being within her that caused people to notice her. Elfrieda wondered if she would ever tell Anna the truth about her background and her circumstances of coming to their home and family. Elfrieda did not dare tell her husband David what she so often hid in her heart and wondered about in relationship to Anna.

Time passed and Anna turned eighteen. The strapping Cornelius Klassen was becoming more handsome in her eyes all the time. He watched her as closely as he dared but the two of them had not yet found the courage to escape for a few minutes to talk in private. The day would come. In the meantime, her father, David, had received the necessary letter of invitation from his relatives in Canada that they had a place in Manitoba for them, if they could come. The Ratzlaffs put out the word that their place and possessions would probably come up for sale; David cautiously approached the authorities for permission to leave Russia. Anna knew now was the time to speak to Cornelius. She had to think of a plan.

The permission from the local authorities, however, must have gotten stuck in the slow and dysfunctional bureaucracy of what was Russia. No response was the only response David lived through day after day. Life dragged on for Anna's family in Neu Samara as they had not been able to obtain land for farming, they had come to this region too late. Those that had come earlier could not hire anyone as farm hands or house servants as drought and severe winters had ruined their ability to make a living. Without work and having had no money in the first place, David had no resources to open a mill or cheese factory as he would have liked.

The only good thing for Anna in these difficult days in Neu Samara was that the Klassens could not leave either, and she and her Cornelius had finally found ways to be alone for brief periods without being discovered by any of the elders of the village or even the prying eyes and certain mischievous and sure-to-be chatty and gossipy village children.

Time passed and finally Cornelius, now an adult, kept his job usually reserved for the teenagers of the village as a cattle herder. Being out in the fields gave him the chance to hunt wild animals to supplement his family's diet and, more importantly, for him, to make and compose music on his harmonica, mostly secret love songs about Anna. But not unlike the biblical shepherd boy, David, Cornelius found himself often, too, writing poems about the wonders of God and His creation. He passed other hours reciting passages he had memorized from the Bible, recalling his lessons from his baptism classes, and reflecting upon the peculiar but rich Mennonite faith and theology of his people. He daydreamed, too, of being a teacher one day, and maybe even a preacher.

With no word regarding permission from the Russian authorities to move to Canada and no increased prospects for success in their community, and there being almost no reason for any joy and celebration left in their community anymore, one night between heavy breathing and much private excitement in a dark corner of a barn hayloft, Anna and Cornelius decided that they should ask her parents if they could get married. Their giggles in the hay, stored above the barn that was itself connected to the rented Ratzlaff home, at the prospect of marriage almost got their surreptitious rendezvous exposed and nearly ruined everything when David stepped into the barn to check on a cow about to calve. The young lovers decided Cornelius would speak to David after church the next Sunday. The week dragged.

"How will you provide for her?" queried David when the nervous Cornelius finally was able to speak to David alone, a full two weeks later, and after more than a little pressure from Anna between kisses in the hayloft. He and she were in passionate Mennonite love.

"The same way all of us provide for ourselves now, with what we have and what we can create from the fields and our gardens," Cornelius said, "and our prayers," he added, quickly, knowing that showing a deep faith always impressed fathers about to give permission for their daughters to marry young men usually too well known to the fathers to be seen too positively. "And we think our families, the village and we, too, could use some joy in this joyless time," added Cornelius at great risk that he might be signalling some frivolity in a community that too much valued serious contemplation and frowned upon too much demonstrated joy. Cornelius' fear of what David might say was not unfounded. Mysteriously some fathers in the village would allow their young daughters to only marry widowers with children, never young men near their own age. Nevertheless, luckily or providentially, David promised he would speak with his wife, Elfrieda, and then with Anna.

Chapter 16
White Rock, Canada — 1996

Suddenly, ten days since first standing at Ben Ruhe's church office door, the mystery woman-child was there again. Again Ben sensed someone's energy and presence in the room before actually hearing or seeing her. This time he let her stand at the doorpost for some time pretending not to know she was there. It was possible she was unable to speak, that she suffered from what was called selective mutism, he thought, realizing with a start he had been unconsciously mulling over their strange encounter the week before when she had seemed both able and not able to speak.

"Hello, my silent friend," he finally said, lifting his head to offer a smile of welcome. "It's good to see you again." He noticed she was wearing brighter clothes than the last time, a pink t-shirt and new white sneakers, and there was a faint hint of eye shadow around her eyes.

"Can we go in the big room again?" she asked, her request came barely above a whisper and in staccato, hesitating after every word.

"Sure," he answered, "let's go." He led the way and both sat where they sat the previous time, he in the front pew, turned sideways toward her, she in the second row, a metre down from him, bent toward the back of the pew in front of her, as if in pain, her eyes so low he could not see them. Her hair was pulled back into a ponytail, with her elbows out she tucked her hands palm down under her knees. Once again he let her lead in her silence. Minutes passed and neither one of them spoke.

Suddenly, barely above a whisper, her voice so small in the big room, she said, "I feel safe in here!"

"That's good," Ben volunteered. More silence. "Safe is something we don't feel often enough in our lives, most of us, I would guess," Ben said then. "You know, I still don't know your name. I don't know how to address you."

"I can't tell you yet," she whispered back. "I will. Someday." She slipped back behind her silent shield for a few more minutes and then raised her head to offer, "I like the stained glass window. It makes the room warm with colour. Do you think God is here?" And then without waiting for an answer she shuddered and said, "I need to go. May I leave?"

"Of course you may. You're always welcome to come here and you can always leave when you like. Go ahead, you know the way out. I'll just stay here for a minute or two after you leave." Ben wanted to test whether she could leave a room ahead of him if she knew he was some distance behind her.

The young woman slid out the far end of the thickly padded church bench and, following the wall closely, made her way to the double exit door of the sanctuary and disappeared around the corner. Ben stayed sitting as he promised. He was no less puzzled with her this time than he was after her first appearance.

A month passed. In that time Ben often wondered about his mystery visitor but the realities of congregational visits, reading to be ready to take a course in abuse counselling, and preparations for another trip to Israel kept him from too much wondering. He was going through some files on his desk when Mrs. Martin, the church secretary, buzzed him on his phone. "Somebody here to see you!" He looked up from his work. For the third time his silent still yet un-named visitor stood at the door.

"I think I can come into your room today," she said, her voice louder than it had been in her first two visits.

Ben had to fight the impulse to get up and move toward her to greet her, but he stayed behind his desk. She had clearly trained him with her palpable brokenness to stay away from her. He wanted to shake her hand, even hug her, but he dared no overtures. Her vulnerability and obvious fragility with such an aura of personal wreckage about her, but yet some enormously suggested strength in her being, made him feel both confused and protective of her. She took one step into his formal space, then two, and with her back to the long dark file cabinet along the wall side-stepped along it until she was next to the front corner of his desk. She was within three feet of him now. She grasped the back of the small armchair standing between the desk and the file cabinet, and lifting and turning it, placed it in such a way that it faced Ben directly across the wide expanse of his desk, now and — nearly always — littered with notes and pens and open books. Ben simply watched what she was doing. It was as if she was arranging her mental space within his space, in order, to expand their short conversations started a couple of months ago, in total words still so brief, so limited. She sat down. For the first time, they were at eye level. Her new behaviour made Ben feel like the room was a scene in a movie, the action in lazy slow motion and screaming high speed, all at the same time.

"My name is Elizabeth." Ben's eyes widened, surprised, he had not anticipated her name would be so forthcoming. "I want to ask you some questions," she added.

"Elizabeth! Elizabeth! Every Elizabeth I have known has been important to me," he said quietly, wanting to let the gravity of her letting him know her name sink in "I've missed you since your earlier visits. It's good to talk with you, and to hear that you have some questions. I hope I can answer them. I have some questions, too, but they can wait. My name is Ben."

"I know your name. This is really hard for me. To, to, come see you, to, to talk to you," she said, the words in staccato, then tailing off. It was obvious she was exerting a great deal of emotional effort to be in his office, to face him, to say the words. Ben waited as he had learned, as she had so quickly taught him.

A familiar silence filled the room. Ben pretended he was busy with something on his desk, hoping it might bring some calm to her, might make it possible for her to speak again.

"You know about God, don't you? And forgiveness?" she asked.

"Some. Maybe a lot. Actually, no matter how much we say we know about God there's a lot more we don't. We professional God people probably like to give the impression that we know quite a bit about God, but I'm not so sure. If we know quite a bit about God it's probably not God we know," Ben smiled. "God's pretty mysterious. So is forgiveness, actually," and then suddenly realizing he was talking too much, an occupational hazard for most ministers, he became silent.

"Does God talk to us?" she queried.

"Has he ever talked to you?" he returned.

"I asked you first."

"Yes, I believe God talks to us, but not always in the ways one would think he talks. God can, I believe, even talk to us in the way you and I are talking to one another right now. Yes, I would say God talks to us. I tell the people in this church that God talks to us through the Bible. But on a more personal note, and I think that's what you're asking, I believe he has talked to me."

Elizabeth shuddered, her hands came up, she looked behind her, became anxious.

"I've taken too much of your time," she stammered. Then she was up, off the chair, out the door, and round the corner with the deftness of an athlete.

Ben would wait for a number of months before he would see her again. In that time it felt to Ben that Elizabeth was not coming back. He often wondered if he had frightened her or if something had happened in her life so she could not come. He had no way of finding her. At times he even wondered if her name really was Elizabeth. He often sighed sitting at his desk when he thought of her. Another Elizabeth had disappeared from his life so many years ago, but that, he knew had been his doing, not hers. Nevertheless, this disappearance he thought he could not completely own.

Chapter 17
Neu Samara, Russia to Barnaul Colony, Siberia to Cherry Creek, Canada — 1896–1937

While David Ratzlaff had seemed not as negatively inclined to Cornelius, overtures regarding Anna's hand as the young man had feared — and had even seemed somewhat positive to Cornelius' surprise — Elfrieda, Anna's mother, must have been not so warm to the idea. It was usually Mennonite fathers who were the gatekeepers of their daughters, but this had not seemed so. David finally reported back to the anxious and hopeful Cornelius that he and Elfrieda agreed with the wedding. But not yet. "You should wait," he suggested, though the tone of his voice was that of an order more than a suggestion. "Anna is only twenty, you know, and we need her help around our house still," he added, as if it were logical.

Anna and Cornelius could not see the logic of it when they next got a chance to be alone, unseen, to talk and they reluctantly agreed that they had no choice but to give the whole thing some time. What they did decide was to make themselves visible as friends and a couple, a brave and very possibly a strategic move given the social realities of their community. They knew that in "whispering" places such as theirs, the local gossips would pressure the parents to let the wedding proceed before something "happened." It always felt to young couples in love in Mennonite Russia that it took a whole village to prevent any premarital inappropriateness.

One year, and then another passed. The hayloft meetings decreased in frequency and intensity as by this time the young couple integrating the meaning of their baptisms into their being, and wanting to live by the rules of their faith community accepted the wisdom of their community. Because they could be seen together at church and at other events, they had opportunities to speak together and plan their future. In the meantime, Elfrieda initiated the creation of a "hope chest" for Anna, mother and daughter together quilted a blanket, collected pretty material for dinner napkins and found a set of candles for the special occasions that would occur in Anna's future home. Elfrieda sometimes let her mind wander to sadness that Anna's real mother could not plan her wedding, and in those moments of silence together, Anna, unaware of what was happening in Elfrieda's mind, simply reflected on the journey her life was taking and wondered what her future held. When would she and Cornelius finally marry? Would they live here in this village or would they suddenly leave for Canada as their families were hoping and praying for? Would she and Cornelius have children? Would God remain deep and wide and alive to her? Would her Christian faith always be vibrant? Like her love for Cornelius?

Anna continued to help Elfrieda in their home and started to assist the local midwife, Mrs. Nikkel, in those hours she could be spared at home. In the absence of doctors in most villages, midwives played enormous medical roles in the Mennonite communities, their involvement often extended beyond birthing and infant care. Anna was an extraordinarily calm person and the women of the village remarked that she was wise beyond her years. She had a quick intelligence and her ability to create conversation, gather knowledge and nurture others earned her special favour in the community. People were drawn to her and she had enormous influence over those around her. Anna bore an unusual charisma, charm, courage and expressed herself with an abrupt forthrightness in her Mennonite community; in a Jewish community people would have been said she had *chutzpah*, and it could be said that without being negative about them, she was very unlike her siblings. Cornelius was often told he was getting "a good one, a special one." He knew he was and it only increased his wish for the day they could get married.

With no movement toward the possibility of a move to Canada or the United States, and feeling he had shown maturity in quietly waiting to be married to Anna for nearly two years, Cornelius again approached David and Elfrieda without having taken the time to tell Anna that he was trying again.

"Thanksgiving is coming," Cornelius said to Anna's parents, "and I not only want to thank God for our survival in this land against many odds, and even for His abundance. I would like to publically thank our Lord for Anna. It feels like I have been waiting for seven years to be married to my beloved like Jacob of the Bible, and the days are dragging, they are not flying by as they were for the Patriarch. May your daughter and I marry immediately?"

"When were you thinking is immediately?" enquired David.

"This Sunday after *Gottesdienst* here in Donskoye!" Cornelius exclaimed.

By five o'clock the village women knew who would make the *zwieback*, who would prepare the sweet fruit *perishky,* and whose husbands would get the little church building ready for such an event beyond the usual. As was the custom everyone in the village would be part of the event. Anna found out how soon she would be married at about the same time *Prediger* Duerksen found out he would need to be ready to conduct a wedding ceremony on Sunday after the morning service. The elderly minister naturally protested saying that a wedding this quick usually implied the couple needed to get married, but Anna did not protest at all when Cornelius breathlessly found her with Mrs. Nikkel talking about a birth they had just attended and told her the good news. Elfrieda moved quickly to set the minister straight regarding his presumptions regarding how quickly weddings should be in the making and clarified for him his role in making a wedding happen by Sunday. With the minister's reticence out of the way, Elfrieda got busy being the mother of the bride-to-be overseeing the women already busy making sure all the details were attended to.

Cornelius' first response to the surprising response from the Ratzlaffs that he and Anna would be getting married so soon was wondering where they would spend their wedding night, where they would live, and, strangely, if there could be *portzelky* at the wedding meal, even though it wasn't New Years Day, the day when raisin fritters were traditionally served in all their homes and at public gatherings. When Cornelius meekly inquired as to the possibility regarding *portzelky,* he was dismissively shushed by the circle of women who had begun to aggressively mind the business of his immediate world and he slunk off to study whose house would be best suited for him and Anna as a married couple: his parents' or Anna's?

The simple though moving wedding ceremony of Anna Ratzlaff and Cornelius Klassen took place immediately after the closing prayer of a Sunday service that seemed endless to Anna. She had sat with her mother on the women's side of the little church house in her wedding dress that a group of village women had hastily assembled and beautifully created from materials pilfered from any number of "hope chests" and secret caches of cloth and buttons. The women had joined their creative forces carefully and thoughtfully knowing that *Prediger* Duerksen and the strong male leadership of the church would chide them, publically if necessary, that modesty must always be the watchword in all Christian women's wear. A wedding dress was to be no exception.

Everyone stayed for *faspa* that made up the reception after the formal marriage ceremony, everyone had helped prepare it, and there was no dance. It was known to the Mennonite young people that in the Jewish villages weddings had meant dances, even if it were the men dancing together in one room, and the women dancing in another, but in the Mennonite village the word 'dance' was very nearly a swear word — there was no dancing. By eight o'clock the lamps and the special candles were all lit in David and Elfrieda's house. Cornelius and Anna shyly excused themselves from the group of relatives from both sides who had gathered in the Ratzlaff *lebensraum* at the front of the home to continue the wedding celebration after the church event earlier in the day, and went to their small bedroom in the Ratzlaff home just off the summer kitchen. Cornelius would never know that he was entering into a committed Christian marriage with a girl who had been born to Jewish parents. How could he, even Anna did not know?

Cornelius and Anna settled in Dolinsk, the neighouring village to Donskoye, and resumed their work — he working with cattle, she with mothers giving birth in any number of Mennonite villages throughout the colony. Within a few weeks of their wedding night Anna knew she was carrying her first child. With the couple anticipating a child their thoughts often turned to the reality of an uncertain future in Neu Samara. They often talked and prayed of being able to move to Canada one day, but they were happy to be married and busy in their church and community. Five children after the first were born to Anna and Cornelius over the next dozen years or so as an uneasy normalcy settled into the life of the Mennonite villages in a country sliding toward increasing anarchy and even a full-fledged a revolution, whether it was known to the Mennonites in their villages and tight communities or not. Then terrible crop failures forced the hand of many. With the situation so dire many of the residents knew they must go to Canada or somewhere else where there was some chance of a better life. The most promising news, however, came from the newly established Mennonite colony of Barnaul in Siberia south of the Novosibirsk that despite its harsh winters boasted deep rich soil for farming. Within months Anna and Cornelius and their six children joined the throng moving east searching yet again for a life of undisturbed faith and economic success. Soon they were creating a new normal in Siberia.

Unfortunately, this new normal, despite the promises of better days ahead in an emerging Russia that would see the communists overturn the old Russian system with the Revolution in 1917 and create new ways of thinking and being, was quickly shown to not be a kinder era than the previous. What the Mennonites feared were the godless fingers of communism and the cancellation of the promises made to them that they would never have to serve in the military, that they could live in their private colonies and that they would always be able to educate their own children as they saw fit. Added to the political and economic changes that were being rumoured and sometimes brutally introduced by the new force of communism and harassment from corrupt officials and undisciplined soldiers, were armed bands of anarchists who would sweep into the villages, as they had in the Ukraine and other parts of the country, only to burglarize, rape and rain down any kind of violence they could think of on vulnerable villages whether they were Mennonite, Jewish or that of any other non-Russian ethnic group that had sought to find a place in Russia. Soon after settling in the Barnaul colony, the Mennonites knew that their dream of peace and quiet, an unmolested faith and economic security would probably not become a reality given the forces of evil they saw everywhere around them.

Cornelius Klassen had become a teacher and a lay minister in the village of Gnadenheim and his wife Anna bore two more children. One of them they named Ruthie. The Klassens and their children including Ruthie, who by the time they were able to leave Russia was not yet a teenager, did not completely escape the horror that became the norm for the scattered peoples of this once great nation.

In time a number of families from the Barnaul Colony were given permission to leave Russia nine years after the onset of the Revolution and as quickly as they could sell their possessions and say farewell to those staying behind, Cornelius and Anna and their children made a harrowing train trip to Moscow, experienced a variety of terrors in the intermediate journey to England, and finally crossed the Atlantic to Quebec City aboard the *HMS Montclare*. Another family on the ship was the Ruhe family from Schönwiese, which was another Mennonite village of the Barnaul Colony. Cornelius Klassen and Franz Ruhe had met on a few occasions at joint churchly meetings and church music events in the colony.

A decade or more later, in a small town in southern Manitoba, Canada, Ruthie Klassen, would marry Jacob Ruhe, the middle son of Franz Ruhe who had had a close friendship and a deep understanding with a Jewish tailor many years before. Not so surprisingly Ruthie loved her husband, Jacob, in ways and words not a lot unlike her mother, Anna, had loved and cared for her Cornelius.

DANNY UNRAU

Chapter 18
White Rock, Canada — 1997

"I think I can tell you more," she enthused, barely through the wide open door of his office one sunny afternoon and although uncharacteristically garrulous she did not say "Hello" and spoke as if no time had passed since their last conversation. Ben was surprised by both her manner and her attendance. Elizabeth had not made an appearance in six months. He had wondered whether she had been travelling, moved, died, or just stopped wanting to see him, or even contemplating God, for that matter.

"I'm listening," Ben smiled.

"I can't tell you everything."

"I don't expect you should."

"I was adopted. That's why I'm such a mess."

"Lots of people are adopted. That doesn't guarantee being messed up, does it?" Ben asked.

"No, but in my case it does. I was born in Germany in 1972. My birth Mom, being single, somehow arranged for me to be adopted by a family in Canada while I was still a newborn. I think even before I was born. That was important to her, that I live in Canada. But in the end she couldn't very much control the kind of family that I would become a part of."

"Did you ever meet her?"

"Yes, twice. I found out about her from my adopted mother against my adopted father's wishes. Mom even secretly paid for me to go back and find my real mother. I was eighteen, and I paid my own way back the second time to spend more time, to know her better, to ask more questions." Elizabeth continued in an unusually animated fashion. Ben thought her to be manic.

"Did your birth Mom welcome you? Was she open to you visiting, and you getting to know each other?"

"Yes! Very much so! She wanted me to come live with her. Especially when she heard that I was - ," Elizabeth's voice trailed off, her demeanor suddenly turned and it seemed she would switch back to the silent and withdrawn person she had been in her earlier visits. "I've said too much already," she stammered, twisting her baseball cap in her hands, looking at the corner of the room and the walls now, rather than at Ben. The frightened child she had been when she first started coming to see Ben had now reappeared in full. It looked like she might bolt for the door.

"After she heard that you were what?" Ben asked, lowering his voice, hoping to prevent her from succumbing to the wracking emotions clearly gathering to overtake her.

"I don't think I can tell you this time," she said, just above a whisper. But she made no move to leave. The familiar silence entered the room, and stayed. Neither Ben nor Elizabeth said anything for what seemed a long time. Her silence, he guessed, was needed for her to gather up the strength required to either get up and leave, or to be able to say more. His silence was to make sure he did not interfere with the emotional storm she was trapped in and needed to overpower. He knew he was required to be silently present. He was surprised by how comfortable he felt waiting with her, in spite of her silence and extreme discomfort. This young woman had an inexplicable effect on him. He felt he could have remained silent for as many hours as she chose to sit there. He felt close to her, strangely connected.

"My adopted father - ," she finally started again. "My adopted father - , " her face darkened as she spit out the words and her body seemed to want to shrink into itself.

Ben froze. The silent pieces of her fears, her extreme caution, her abject skittishness started to come together for him. Here was the explanation that he had wondered about, but knew he could never ask about without her leading him into it. His stomach tightened up. It must be her adopted father, he now thought, who was the cause of her conspicuous pain, the reason she could not let a man walk closely behind her, the reason she sidled along the walls when entering rooms she had not been in before, or her jittery movements when alone with someone, a man, at least, in a room or a small confined space. Ben did not want to let himself imagine what horrors her adopted father might have visited upon her in her growing up years. He could feel anger rising in his chest. He wanted to protect her, even from the recollection.

Elizabeth sat silently again, hunched over. She was biting her lip and she had her hands pressed together almost as if praying. She closed her eyes tightly, and then unlocked her hands. She opened her eyes quickly, shot what seemed a frightened look at Ben, and seeing he had not moved, fixed him with a bold look, for the first time not averting them quickly.

"He was a Nazi. My adopted father. A Canadian Nazi. There weren't many in Canada after World War II, at least I don't think there were, but the man who adopted me was a Nazi. He had uniforms, helmets, swastikas, armbands, whips, boots, everything. In boxes in the attic. When no one else but me was around he would put on his uniform. Even my mother didn't know. I don't think she knew. He said it was our secret. He started by showing me his things. His mementoes. Then—!" She started to weep, and then continued, "how does it happen that a little girl from Germany gets a Nazi for an adopted dad in Canada? What kind of God would - ?"

Her words tailed off, she took a breath, and continued. "When I met my birth mom in Germany she said that her father too — I have to go now!" By now Elizabeth's jaw was quivering, her hands were again tightly fisted, she was fighting back sobs. She stood up and ran out of Ben's office.

Ben did not move from his chair to watch her go. He sat wondering. About her story. About what horrors she must have endured growing up. About her real mother back in Germany. He was somehow aware that he did not hear her car start up on the street in front of the church as he sat lost in his thoughts, his own emotions. And then she was at the door again.

"I need to tell you something else. I need to tell you!" she said in little more than a whisper, but with some determination and emphasis. "My birth mother's father, he, too, was a Nazi. She told me herself. This last time I went to Germany to see her I started to tell her about my Canadian dad, and what he did to me. She started to cry. She cried a long time. She said she was sorry. I didn't know all the reasons, at first. I asked her over and over to tell me why she was crying. It was just as hard for her to say things as it is for me. Do we inherit mannerisms and stuff like emotions and other characteristics from our parents even if we didn't grow up with them? She finally told me she was crying because she'd given me up. About writing an adoption agency in Canada, about letting a Canadian adoption agency find someone near Winnipeg, and then sending me to them to raise me. She said she had her reasons then. And then she cried some more.

I don't remember exactly but I think it was the next day she told me that her father, Walter, my grandfather, I guess, he would have been, had been a soldier, a guard at Dachau. The concentration camp close to Munich. He was a Nazi guard in a concentration camp. I guess I was going to get a Nazi in my life no matter what," Elizabeth laughed. It was the first time

Ben had heard her laugh. But it was a humourless, dry laugh. She seemed now to have no tears. She stood up as if to leave the room, but slowly this time, as if she did not want to go.

Ben stayed sitting but asked, "May I hold you, Elizabeth? May I hug you?"

"Yes!" she whispered. "Please!"

Ben slipped from behind his desk and enveloped her in his arms. With her face sideways against his chest he held her for a long time. Tears rolled down his cheeks and dropped into her hair. She stood against him with her arms straight down by her sides. He could not tell whether she was weeping as well, or whether her emotions had simply shut down. How long they stood in his office this way he did not know. It seemed a considerable time.

At last she said, "I need to go," pulled herself free, and left the room. Ben sat down in the chair that Elizabeth usually sat in and let his mind wander. He sat a long time after he heard her car move away from the curb outside his office window and long after he had heard everyone else leave the building.

Chapter 19
Cherry Creek, Canada — 2000

Ruthie Ruhe had indeed survived the birth, and even the growing up of her fifth child, Ben. But gall bladder problems, kidney dysfunction, low-grade depression, and any number of other medical maladies, both large and small, racked her body, ate at her emotions, and tore at her soul. Her children respected her and loved her in their own way, but became largely deaf to the ailments she referred to in so many of her conversations. Fixated on illnesses, she talked endlessly about what ailed her as she aged. She even told them *ad nauseam* of the diseases her neighbours and the women of her church lived with, and what surgeries the person who happened to be walking past her home in the morning when they were sitting at breakfast had had. And then came the report of the meeting at which the doctor uttered the C word — cancer. Ruthie Ruhe had cancer. Cancer. On top of her chronic anemia.

While her family had previously and increasingly ignored her talk of illness and operations, doctors and medical minutia, it now rallied round her on her sick bed. After being mostly ignored in her illnesses through so much of her life, Ruthie Ruhe finally got the attention she had been desperate for in the past, in sharing her infirmities.

Talking about ones illnesses and aches and pains seemed to be a family trait. It was remembered that many of her siblings and even her otherwise irrepressible mother, Anna, who had been a kind of medical practitioner in her own right as a young woman back in Russia, had spoken often in her declining years about being unwell. Many of those who lived alongside the complainants saw the distress words as little more than manipulative techniques employed to gain some sympathy and notice. One of Ruthie's brothers was dubbed "*Ich bin krank* Uncle Jasch" by his nieces and nephews because that was what he always said when asked how he was, "*Ich bin krank! (I am sick).*" Jasch had had a headache from his late twenties or so, he was happy to tell anyone, until just two weeks before he died, still looking hale and hearty for a man of his ninety-some years. Family members affectionately and tearfully joked that he died when the doctors found a medication that took his headache away after all this time because he simply did not know how to live without it. Nevertheless, Ruthie's children, finally believing that she was truly ill, no longer ignored her talk of ailments. They gathered round her bed when she was in hospital and when she was able to be at home. They visited, fussed, spent time talking, reading, remembering and caring.

Jacob, her retired immigrant farmer husband and longtime partner, reignited the domestic skills of cooking and cleaning that he had learned as a youngster, being the only son among many brothers who, by his own account, would ever lift a hand to help out his mother when he was a child. She too had been chronically ill. Now he set to caring for his wife and managing the house they lived in.

Jacob had become a true and proud Canadian in the decades he had lived in the country his parents had brought him to as a teenager. For most of his adult years a struggling farmer, but a good neighbour, he had even, for a time, been the chairman of the local schoolboard of the one-room country school that was the center and the focus of the farming community in which he and Ruthie had lived and raised their children in. Among his tasks of chairing the school board was recruiting, interviewing and hiring teachers for the community school. It was a significant achievement for a man who had only reached Grade six in Canada himself, and that in less than one year of sitting in a classroom where he understood almost nothing of the English the teacher was speaking. In his vibrant storytelling he often told his children of having been a very shy and humiliated fourteen-year-old in Grade one, and speaking not a word of the language and despite his age and size, he was made by his teacher to squeeze into one of the tiny desks reserved for the Grade one students. There was no other way. After all, he was in the first grade. That first graders sit in Grade one desks was the unalterable rule of the first and only Canadian teacher Jacob ever had.

He reported that he moved through the grades rapidly in that year as he was learning to speak English, and only once argued with the teacher about the lunacy of the silent "k" on the word "knife" and by the end of that first year in school he was proudly sitting in a Grade six desk, and was given a pass to Grade seven on his final report card. Despite the fact that his earliest experience of school in Canada was mostly a demeaning one, Jacob held onto a near reverence for education right up to his death. He remembered aloud and often, with deep regret, that he was never able to begin the seventh grade given the economic realities of the times. The dire near-starvation status of his family made it necessary that he find work that second year of their being in Canada. Off to work he went, hiring on with threshing crews working from farm to farm, cutting wood for people needing fire wood or oak fence posts, and doing odd jobs in the community until he was old enough, and found the means to rent, and then finally, with a loan from a sympathetic businessman in the area, to buy his own land to farm when he was a young adult and already married.

DANNY UNRAU

His marriage to Ruthie Klassen was strong. They squabbled some, to be sure. She was bright and often felt she did not get the chance to do what she might have been capable of doing had she not married a poor farmer and had so many children. Her emotions were often ragged, she was stressed and high strung, even hysterical at times. Jacob Ruhe's demeanour, on the other hand, was more to the calm and cool, but when he knew Ruthie might disagree with him over some issue he would often follow his own whims even if they had discussed some compromise. Registering Ben as Ben for his birth certificate rather than Bobby was not the only time Jacob had gone against something the two of them had previously agreed upon.

In Ruthie's years of being ill, and as he had retired from farming, Jacob's domestic skills transitioned into caregiving, and at that he became quite extraordinarily skilled. Besides cooking and cleaning and managing the home, he learned to administer pain-relieving massages for his bedsore wife. In her final months he spent entire days by her hospital bedside, following a best bedside ritual of intermittent reading, talking, and being silent.

Son Ben, who often came back to Manitoba to see his aging parents, observed their interaction. He noticed that though his mother might remain completely still, eyes shut, throughout entire days in her hospital bed, she seemed always to revive herself for a parting conversation with her Jacob before he left the hospital at day's end to spend the night at home. In those parting conversations Jacob would lean over his wife's bed and speak straight into her suddenly wide open eyes. Seeing his parents' connection from where he was standing at the hospital door, Ben was struck, and intrigued, by how intense, how animated their conversation was, especially considering that she had lain quiet and nearly immobilized all day. There was a singular intensity and flow of energy between them as they talked in these moments as they ended their days together, in spite of his mother's deteriorating condition and his dad's bedside inactivity. He saw the deep fervour in their relationship, their passion and affection for one another. He felt he was watching scenes in a movie.

Driving his Dad home after one of these very intense farewells, Ben remarked at the depth and passion that he saw in his parents' exchange. He asked the elderly Jacob if that intensity had always been there, adding that if it had been, he had certainly not been aware there was so much vitality in their relationship. "You finally noticed," old Jacob smiled in response. "You young folk think you have a corner on love."

While she lay in the hospital getting weaker, with the cancer that she was now fighting, Ruthie's doctors prescribed pain management methods. Pills had always been the cause of a certain level of trauma of their own — she always claimed that her stomach simply could not abide the invasions of most medications — hence, she insisted that chemotherapy was out of the question. Radiation, she was told by medical practitioners, was a valid means to make her remaining time more comfortable. At set junctures in her medical downturn she was ambulanced to the radiation clinic for treatments. Whether the treatments were successful or not, was never known; that they did terrible damage was no mystery for she suffered severe radiation burns when a radiologist technician made a serious error one day during treatment.

Surprisingly, especially to her doctors, Ruthie soldiered on after the episode of the extreme radiation burning. It seemed in having been ill so long she had acquired significant skills of pain management, endurance and survival. Her case became known to the hospital staff and the wider medical community; she should never have survived the doses of radiation that she received, but she did.

Chapter 20
Dachau, Germany — 1942–1945

Walter Becker's position at Dachau remained unchanged. While his colleagues were recognized, re-trained, rewarded, transferred and promoted for their exemplary work, Walter, though not being formally criticized for his contribution, stayed where he was as the shift-commander of the *Scheisskommando* of the Dachau Concentration Camp. That he remained in his position had, of course, huge consequences in relationship to Sophia and the people she connected with, and even to Walter as he continued, barely aware of it, down a road of inner transformation. He never learned, even later in life, to articulate what really happened to his soul and spirit that last year, and especially those last months in Dachau managing the Jewish *sauber* women of the camp, but he did know beyond a doubt for the rest of his life that something of significance occurred there. A little of what happened inside of Walter that year was surmised and not forgotten by Sophia, either, for the rest of her days. The two of them, though, would never ever get to speak of it with one another. In camp they had communicated on a number of occasions, formally around the work, but the situation was such that they were never able to have the kind of conversation that anyone would ever call normal. The distance between their positions in camp was too great. What the two of them might have shared years later after the horror of the camp was behind them would most likely have been mystical and spiritual and possibly with some warmth given how Sophia's final day at Dachau unfolded.

The war dragged on. More and more people were brought to Dachau, more came through those iron gates of the horrifically insulting familiar *Arbeit Macht Frei* greeting every day than even the most imaginative killers in the place could liquidate in a day. The numbers of newcomers themselves carried the death of their spirits and the demise of hope within their beings as they shuffled into its premises.

Walter sensed that the war was moving toward its end. The spirit of the Führer's hoped for one-thousand year reign was dying, and while no one dared to mention that something was afoot, a change was coming in this great land. Pride and confidence gave way to sadness, and a sense of hopelessness began to erode the soul of Germany. Walter noticed this change in his own particular community when he went home on weekends on leave. Farmers started talking more about farming and less about the war; women started to fuss about their families again, and volunteered less and less at community war events. It all seemed to matter less. Alongside a natural war weariness was the growing awareness that something had gone very wrong in Germany again.

On the weekends that he was given leave from Dachau to visit his family at Biegelhof, Walter started again to regularly attend the little Mennonite church at Horsbach that had been so much a part of his life as a child. Its tiny institutional life breathed a vibrant life-giving message into his spirit again and started to supplant the specter of death of Dachau that had wanted to ravage his soul. While the people of Horsbach had not resolved the struggle between desiring a stronger Germany as articulated by Hitler and their contention that war was outside of God's will, just the fact that they read the Bible and prayed together without making any direct application to the situation in some way spoke against the horror. Walter did not realize at first that he enjoyed being in this little conservative church gathering again on the Sundays that he could attend as it gently laid its healing hand on the spirit of death and disconnect that had invaded his soul and needed reviving, resorting, resettling, and cleansing, he would reflect in later years. While the traditional beliefs of his childhood were still largely cold to him, Walter began to realize there was something larger in this gathering, in these people, in the spirit of the place, and soon, even though indefinably but increasingly real within himself, as he sat and sang the old German hymns and listened to the stern preaching of the teaching elder. Walter's heart, his identity, increasingly craved a connection that he could not place but was announcing itself in his soul like the changing skies and the shifting winds of a coming rain. It was nearing the middle of the 1940s and he could not yet see how soon the wars raging around him and within him would conclude.

It was at the church service at Horsbach that Walter first noticed Greta. He wondered how he had not really noticed her before. She was the daughter of another Mennonite farmer of their small faith community, and his sudden notice of her somehow reinforced the peace and rightness of this little religious community and its simple yet complex narrative. It startled and interested him that she reminded him of Sophia, the *Scheisskommando* woman he oversaw back at Dachau. The two women were years apart in age and their situations, of course, could not have been more different, but he sensed a similar spirit and a centredness and a solidity in both of them that drew attention to the woman wrapped around such soul. Often when he sat on the men's side of the meetinghouse on Sundays and glanced sideways at Greta, when he risked the gossip if it be seen, he thought he saw Sophia. This parallel response to these two women in Walter made him more curious about Sophia when he was back on shift at Dachau after a weekend away, but the weekend itself and the activity and the thinking and the reflection of the church experience only made his work more difficult. And these feelings of disorientation and conflictedness that he still adhered to in his head, only complicated Walter's days and nights, his very existence, more and more. He dared not reveal his growing discontent in his work to his commanders at Dachau, he hardly dared admitting it to himself, and one day completely surprised himself when he found that he was silently praying for an escape from this life. He found himself yearning for a life that felt like what he felt sitting in the little church in Horsbach. That feeling was fanned by more longing and mental flights of fancy about Greta. Walter began to wonder how long he could last in Dachau. In that wondering his mind increasingly joined with the minds of his people back at Horsbach.

Luckily, perhaps, his workload increased as the population of the camp grew. For a minor concentration camp commander, Walter worked exceptionally hard. He was committed to keeping his *Scheisskommando* unit intact, especially under its mystical and informal spiritual peer leader, Sophia. He risked his own safety by secretly leaving bonbons and packages of tea for her and her cohorts his first few days back at work after having been on leave.

Soon Walter was going for walks with Greta when he was home on weekends. He told her of Sophia and she started to knit socks and embroidered handkerchiefs for Sophia and her partners. The connection between the Jewish prisoner and the Mennonite girlfriend intensified for Walter within his mental affections, and even his identity as a person. One day he took another risk. He told Sophia about Greta as he presented her the orders for the day and slipped a package of socks under the papers. Sophia responded with a hint of interest in her eyes, whether to the story of Greta or that a guard was speaking to her as a person, was not clear. These two women, worlds apart, who would probably never meet, were being pulled and held together by a chord beyond human defining. Walter moved between these two feminine centres in his disconnected living. Nor was there ever a conscious disconnect between his mysterious compassion for the elderly Jewish woman and his Mennonite Christian sensibility which should have been jaded by the so much twisted Christian teaching and the propaganda of his pseudo-Christian Germany in the years leading up to the war under the monster Hitler and his beastly henchmen.

Typhus began to ravage the camp as word of the worsening war effort for the Germans began to be whispered. Work became more difficult for Walter as hygiene became even worse in the camp than before. As if such could be possible. This, of course, made life even more difficult for Sophia as she and her team carted disease-infested wastes out of the camp all day long, day after day. Walter became almost desperate in his surveillance of Sophia's safety and wellbeing, even though he had only really spoken to her as a human being that one time he had slipped her the socks. He knew all too well the dangers of over familiarity as even the commanders were watched. No one was safe. Eroding loyalty could not be hidden for long in the paranoid system that the Nazi's had erected. Walter was probably spared detection despite some earlier suspicions by the fact that all the Third Reich stood for seemed to be headed for destruction by this time, and Walter's superiors were too busy creating safety nets for themselves to worry about a lesser commander.

On a spring weekend early in 1945, Walter asked Greta to marry him when the war would end, adding, "If we survive." She smilingly agreed. Before his leave was over Greta gave Walter another pair of socks she had knitted to give to Sophia when he went back to Dachau; spontaneously Walter bravely, and possibly foolishly for everyone, late that same night recruited three of his trusted Mennonite church brothers to be in the forest outside of Dachau one evening that next week to spirit Sophia and the rest of her *Scheisskommando* team of women away from Dachau and back to their little Horsbach church some one-hundred kilometres away. That they had allowed themselves to be recruited spoke of something bigger than Walter's human powers of persuasion and his appeal to duty and dignity. It was near the beginning of April, 1945. Two days before Dachau was liberated, men with their faces covered with bandanas stepped out from behind the trees in the woods as Sophia "and her girls" dumped their loads in the forest, hissing to her to come quickly. She ran as best she could in the makeshift shoes tied over her new socks into the woods with the men she unequivocally trusted, the others stumbling after her. Walter, who had assigned himself as the primary guard on this trip into the woods that evening, saw her run; he smiled and even thought this act of compassion was worth dying for before his mind went back to Greta. He ached to be with her. Sophia hid with her Mennonite saviours for a week but never saw Walter again before these same men who had rescued her were able to contact the Jewish resistance and take her into deeper safety elsewhere in the country. Walter never heard of her again.

The War screamed to an ending. German soldiers were rounded up, and some of the guards at Dachau were even killed by the camp liberators outraged at what they found when the *Arbeit Macht Frei* gate was finally broken through. Walter quietly drifted back to his community after a short time of incarceration as a POW. In time he married Greta, took over the family farm, became a deacon in the church at Horsbach, discovering he had morphed into becoming a true believer, and tried to forget the war and Dachau. He and Greta had three children and among them a daughter named Liesbett.

Greta sometimes asked Walter if he thought Sophia had survived, if he wondered where she might be and what had become of her. His eyes welled up with tears hearing these questions but he never said much more than a few words about his time at Dachau, not even when his children asked him years later. Neither to defend himself nor explain anything. He chose to remain silent. He thought he deserved any misunderstanding that might come his way for his having served in Dachau in the first place and that kept him, too, from excusing himself by telling how he had "saved" Sophia during her days in the camp, and in the end arranging her escape. He took his thoughts and true feelings to his grave; even Greta knew little of what his soul carried from those days. His settled spirit was no more calm anywhere else than when he sat in Church at Horsbach. His most difficult times were when years later his daughter, Liesbett, attacked him for his past. But his difficult was not because he would not defend himself but because of her harshness. He wished he could spare his daughter her harsh singlemindedness. He understood how much damage that much negative passion could do to its host.

Chapter 21
Seattle, USA – 2002

In the medical circles that watch aberrant medical phenomena such as radiation burn survival, Ruthie Ruhe became somewhat of a celebrity. Research doctors started to call and even write her, all curious about her uncommon durability and her condition, which seemed so remarkable despite her being mostly bedridden and more in the hospital than at home. Subsequently, she was asked to participate in a unique study of radiation burn survivors that would include, among other studies, an extensive DNA appraisal by the renown researcher, Dr. Levy Koffman, and a team of researchers working out of his innovative medical research centre in Seattle.

The study included the expected intensive interviews and conversations, the taking of blood samples, and a battery of scans, none of which were overly invasive or discomforting for Ruthie. The researcher and his assistants worked diligently at analyzing her medical history. Her place of birth, all her countries of domicile, countries visited, with time spent and dates noted, illnesses, medical issues known to her family of origin and throughout her biological system, eating habits, exercise regimes, highs and lows in weight as to age and situation, births, miscarriages, onset of menopause, medicines taken and bones broken. Everything and anything was noted and checked and double-checked. Research assistants studied the community histories of the peoples and places where she had lived and visited over the span of her entire life for whatever could possibly be known regarding medical and biological characteristics, uniquenesses and anomalies.

The lion's share of the study, however, was aimed at a deep analysis of Ruthie's biological family. Her detailed family tree was diagramed and a genogram was drawn up, and as much information as possible was tagged to these working charts. Relationships of every imaginable kind were noted, every type and class of connections and observations were made. Any of Ruthie's relatives who might have some information and possibly helpful memories were contacted to fill in the blanks of what she could not remember or seemed not to know details of that might be of interest and relevance to the study.

The researchers were very interested, of course, in knowing of Ruthie's birth and early childhood in Siberia, and of her parents. They worked with a Mennonite historian to create a profile of the village in which she was born, and sought just as diligently to determine where her parents were born and grew up. Oral histories of parents, siblings, birth order, childhood diseases and deaths, medical care and illnesses in the village before she emigrated to Canada were all explored from remaining contemporaries. The rare records of Mennonite archives in Winnipeg and Kitchener were investigated. These files were studied and used as guides for wider conversations and further study. Letters of enquiry were sent to research centres in St. Petersburg, Russia.

Ruthie was stimulated by this interest in the story of her early family life, and predictably, in all the interest in her health issues. Finally somebody, and somebody important, a doctor and all his friendly assistants, were really interested and listening. Her children noted that she recalled stories and events and gladly volunteered as much information as she could muster. Despite her weakening body, her spirits soared.

The researchers assigned to Ruthie dug up records of illnesses and maladies in Russian born Mennonites and searched in the few Siberian sources and Ukrainian records they were able to locate, though such information was hard to find and proved to be limited in value once found and deciphered. Nowhere, though, could the research place any correlation between what Ruthie's general diagnoses plus ability to combat the radiation burn she had experienced and what the records of others in her Mennonite heritage revealed. The team members met in Dr. Koffmann's office in Seattle from time to time to share their findings. After they had compiled and interpreted their data to date, they finally concluded that they had nothing of any help in understanding either Ruthie's pre-cancerous illnesses, her anemic condition, or her remarkable immunity to massive over radiation.

"We're missing something," Dr. Levy Koffmann mused, reluctant to drop this particular research project. "I'd like to keep this study going," he added, "but our funding will run out after I report our progress, or the lack of it. Unless we can find a stream within our work that justifies ongoing study we will have to wrap it up. But I still think we're missing something."

"We've set up a base line for Mrs. Ruhe from our DNA work, and run it through the computer," volunteered Linda, one of the younger graduate student researchers, "surely there's a lot of new money for more DNA study given the new interest in that. The DNA of Mennonites, especially those with a Russian connection coming out of that country in the 1920s isn't a huge bank yet. We'd have to do a lot more foundational work to get to the specifics we're looking for in this study, but that's something we could do."

"Why don't we do some wider DNA studies of her kind of anemia, *fanconi anemia*. Our subject had a mysterious cross-reference into some of the larger and emerging data banks of matrilineal or maternally inherited mitochondrial DNA studies. We might find something," another of the researchers named Mary suggested. "We are dealing with a female subject. Maybe we need more of a view to our subject's gender rather than just pursuing a concentrated look at the people group research we've been doing. We know that mtDNA is a record of what is passed from a mother to her children and maybe, just maybe, we'll link into a haplogroup as we run the data. It might signal something we haven't thought of, or some connection we've missed."

"Well, we're certainly missing something," mused Dr. Koffmann again. "Let's see if we can squeeze a little more out of this data before we give up."

So the research team decided to have some of its researchers follow the wide-ranging suggestions emanating from their meeting and agreed to e-mail one another if anything turned up. Most of them turned to the other projects they were working on. Linda, the researcher who had suggested the maternally inherited mitochondrial DNA (mtDNA) study, put herself to that specific task, mindful that unlike nuclear DNA which is inherited from both parents when genes get rearranged in the creation of a new entity, there is virtually no change in mtDNA from parent to offspring, at least not discernibly over many generations. "Some information or patterns could thus be traced back," she said as she and colleague sat in front of a microscope and a computer, both of them idle. Her partner left Linda to her mtDNA musings and started an internet search of *fanconi anemia* to see whether there were any studies that correlated DNA research and any forms of anemia.

Weeks passed. Initially the mtDNA study on banks of the Internet and saved data studies produced nothing worth noting. Then all at once Linda was alerted to something. She had programmed her computer to run columns of DNA strings, what to the uninitiated would have resembled what filled the screen at times in the movie *The Matrix*. The combinations of numbers had been scrolling columns of green numbers on the screen of one of her computers for days without a hitch. Suddenly the running screen stopped as it had been programmed to do if some kind of a preset match was ever found. The numbers on the screen stood still. Linda clicked on the highlighted string. There it was. A clear correlation between the DNA sample taken from the subject, Ruthie Ruhe, and what Linda was looking for stood side by side. Linda clicked back into the data to see if it matched the information taken from Mennonite or Siberian histories. The tagline, however, under which the highlighted and computer stopping information was bunched, was a mystery to her. There should be no match here, she thought; there must be some mistake. The information on the screen was geographically accurate in being from eastern Russia or Siberia, but it came from a completely different people group. Linda manually checked the similarities in the long rows of digital information to make sure there was truly a match and that the stoppage was not simply a temperamental computer thinking it had done enough for one day. The information matched. There was a real correlation between their subject's mtDNA and the string caught by the scan. But it still made no sense to Linda. No matter how she reviewed her scientific method and thinking paradigms, the results seemed impossible so she switched to thinking "outside the box," sought another way to analyze what she was seeing. But it made no sense that there should be a match in the mtDNA of the subject with the mtDNA string standing still on Linda's screen. Finally she noted and verified the information, saved it to a USB drive, and turned once again to explore the profile of the mtDNA that had just been identified as being a match to their radiation burned survivor, Ruthie Ruhe.

DANNY UNRAU

Linda thought she should e-mail Dr. Koffmann immediately, but changed her mind. This was too puzzling to bother him just yet. He would ask questions to which she had no answers. That night she stayed late in the lab mostly staring at the screen as it ran through information about the DNA string that had come up as a match. Information began to compile itself. What was so puzzling to Linda was that standing on her split screen was a DNA match between a Mennonite subject and a Jewish subject. Biologically, socially and religiously, of course, she knew these were mutually exclusive people groups.

Linda knew that Jewish and Mennonite groups in Russia and Siberia in the nineteenth and early twentieth centuries married almost exclusively within their own ethnic and faith communities. She knew of no data, no records, to indicate that individuals from these two groups intermarried; no children with overlapping DNA would thus be found. But here Linda had in front of her on her computer screen, which could only report, not lie or conjecture or project, the mtDNA markers of a Mennonite subject found only in Jewish subjects. It was time to call Dr. Koffmann; an E-mail would not do.

"I've got something very puzzling here, Dr. Koffmann," Linda said, barely saying hello when he picked up the phone.

"And how's that?" he asked.

"I have the mtDNA markings of our Mennonite subject, Ruthie Ruhe, with the radiation burns, but her DNA has the clear markings of a Jewish mother or grandmother. Something doesn't fit here. I've never seen a match between these two people groups before. It shouldn't happen. Neither the Jews nor the Mennonites were inclined to intermarry, especially in Russia in the last two centuries. Either our study is flawed or we've got something here that needs some hard looking at."

"Did you rerun the samples, or check whether you entered the data correctly?" asked Dr. Koffmann.

"I've checked and doublechecked. There's no doubt that this Mennonite woman has Jewish mtDNA markings."

"Well, Linda, that's why we do research. To discover surprises and find new truths," chuckled Dr. Koffmann. "Let's see if we can contact our Mennonite — maybe Jewish — Ruthie Ruhe to see if she's up to letting us dig into her family history again to find out if there's a Jewish woman there who became pregnant cavorting in the hayloft somewhere with a young Mennonite stud or lonely married man looking for some intimate comfort while his wife was busy with a baby. These things did sometimes happen!" he laughed.

"That would be too simple," countered Linda, "But something is definitely new here. Did you still have any meetings planned with Mrs. Ruhe?"

"I wasn't planning any, but I did tell her I might want to get back to her. Can you get her contact particulars, and leave them on my desk for tomorrow, Linda? I might want to revisit some simple oral research with her. We'll have a look at what this Mennonite girl knows about Jews in her family history, about Jews in her exclusively Mennonite village in Siberia, or where her family may have hailed from before they moved to that end of Russia so long ago."

Chapter 22
White Rock, Canada – 1997

Ben happened to be standing at his office window when Elizabeth pulled her car up in front of the Church office. He noticed that she nearly stopped directly in front of the office but then, seemingly, upon second thought, rolled the car forward a few car lengths along the curb as if to be hidden from the office windows by the high and huge rhododendron in the middle of the lawn. Ben watched her get out of the car and hesitantly move toward the sidewalk leading up to the main door of the building. Obviously in the same state of conflicted mind walking as driving she stopped part way up the sidewalk and half turned to go back, but then turned and continued toward the door again. Ben waited. When she came through the front door, he was standing in front of the main office and he greeted her as enthusiastically as he dared.

"Hello stranger. Good to see you. It's been a few weeks since you were last here. You okay?

"Yeah!" she said, barely above a whisper, obviously thrown off by the surprise of him seeing her first, and she not getting time to prepare herself outside his office. "Can we go in your office?" as if on this day she felt more afraid outside the office than in.

"Sure! No big room God visit today?"

"I don't think God talks. I don't know if He listens. Or can hear. Or even exists for me, I guess," she said a little breathlessly. Her shoulders dropped and her eyes went to the floor.

"Now that's a switch. You've usually felt some sense of peace around the idea of God. What's happened?" Ben asked.

"You tell me. You're the guy who knows God. You're the one who teaches people their perception of God."

"But it's not our perception that creates or uncreates God, Elizabeth, it's just our perception that helps determine what the relationship between him and us will be. God can neither be created nor destroyed. That's what they used to say about matter in chemistry class. And I daresay God is even more than matter"

"I didn't come to talk to you about God today," she said, cutting him off, her voice, louder than usual and sounding peevish and impatient.

"But you did come to see me today, and that's good."

"We'll see." she said, "May I sit down?" They were in his office by this time.

Ben pulled a chair from the computer desk and set it directly in front of and facing his desk. Then he moved around behind his large desk to give her the usual safety zone between the two of them before he sat down in his chair facing the empty one he had placed. Elizabeth waited until he was seated before she sat down. She seemed on edge, but deliberate in her actions as well, as if she had prepared them. Rehearsed them.

"I felt I could say some more things today, but - " she started. "But now that I'm here I don't know anymore. It's really hard."

"Lots of things are hard to say. That doesn't always mean we shouldn't say them, that they're to be avoided. But take your time," Ben volunteered.

"I don't want to hurt you."

"Hurt me? How could you hurt me?" Ben countered. He realized immediately, and too late to cut off the suggestion in his retort that she was incapable of hurting him, or that he was incapable of being hurt. He should not give her the impression that he was the strong one and she the weaker. He saw her wince, and, for a second, knew that he might have broken the spell that had given her the strength and the resolve to talk today. He knew, from experience, that any deflection could send her scurrying for the exit.

"I could hurt you. I've hurt lots of people."

"I'm sure you could. I shouldn't have said what I said," Ben said quietly. "But I've only seen a gentle person in you all the times you've been here, Elizabeth. I've seen a frightened person. A shy person. A broken person, too. But always I've seen a gentle one. I wonder who that person is that you say can hurt others, and I wonder where she is now?"

"This isn't what I came to talk about either!" she interrupted. "I have something to tell you."

"The floor's yours." Ben waved his hand, palm up, trying to be inviting without being condescending or argumentative. She seemed argumentative, and that was new.

In that second, though, her eyes had dropped to the floor and she seemed unable to look up for some long moments. She leaned so far forward in her chair her head protruded over the front of Ben's desk, she moved it from side to side, not to see what was on the desk right below her eyes but rather looking at the wall below the window on the one side or over into the coat rack in the corner on the other, where the Jewish prayer shawl and Palestinian *keffiyeh* hung together. Her looking around the room was avoidance, clearly she could not make eye contact with Ben today.

"You're my dad!" she blurted out suddenly, and then again, "You're my dad!"

Chapter 23
Seattle, USA to Cherry Creek, Manitoba — 2002

Dr. Koffmann and Linda Davids caught an early morning flight out of Seattle to Calgary and then on to Winnipeg. In Winnipeg they rented a car and headed south and west. During the nearly three hours of the road trip to their destination, the doctor and his assistant read the brightly painted welcome signs at the edges of small prairie towns such as Fannystelle and St. Claude, all huddled around grain elevators, safely passed through the RCMP radar trap set up in the driveway of the L&J's Drive-Inn at Treherne, and smiled at the larger-than-life, out-of-place plastic camel gazing toward the sand hills at Glenboro. They discussed the case they were studying and a strategy for their upcoming meeting with Ruthie Ruhe. Linda remarked that while they had opened up a new mystery there was little hope that they would solve the questions their research posed regarding Ruthie Ruhe's condition. Though, she hoped, they could find enough new information to rationalize keeping the study going; they were spending considerable funds making this trip so it needed to produce something of worth.

As they entered the town of Cherry Creek, its perimeter showing the usually prairie town trappings, farm equipment and fertilizer dealers — tractors and huge tanks all in straight lines — Linda glanced at the piece of paper with the map she had drawn while talking to Jacob Ruhe on the phone when she had called to make arrangements for an in-home consultation a few days earlier. They drove past the Busy Bee hamburger stand, between the collegiate and the graveyard with its huge Manitoba maple trees, and turned left onto the first street as her sketch directed. The row of prairie town bungalows differed only slightly from one another. The number of the Ruhe's house came into view; Linda turned the rental car up and into the driveway. An inside door and then an outer screen door opened before the car had even stopped and a white-haired, slightly balding, elderly gentlemen stepped out onto the landing. He beckoned them to come in. It was clear by his handshake, the droop of his shoulders, and the sparkle in his eyes that Jacob Ruhe was both a little intimidated and somewhat exhilarated by the visit of these "very important" people, as he had described his expected visitors to one of his daughters on the phone the evening before. Dr. Levy Koffmann and Linda Davids stepped into the front room.

Mrs. Ruhe sat queen-like in a large naugahyde covered easy chair facing the door, her face paper-white, her body covered to her throat by a multi-coloured crocheted, afghan. As the visiting researchers' eyes adjusted to the dim light in the house, Ruthie Ruhe stretched her hand out from under her afghan to shake the hand of the visitors. She had met Dr. Koffmann in Seattle at the height of the research a couple of years earlier, but she said she did not think she had met Ms. Davids before. Jacob Ruhe disappeared into the kitchen to put water on for tea. He opened a package of chocolate cookies he had bought at the grocery store for these special guests. He was partial to medical people; he had often told his children that had he been able to get an education instead of farming he would have wanted to become a pharmacist.

The visitors and Ruthie made small talk while they waited for Jacob to join them. The conversation shifted from the weather to how she was feeling and then on to the latest word on her condition. The happy patient employed some of the medical language her sharp mind had noted, memorized and retained from her many years of medical issues and numerous hospitalizations, words she could not use with her family. By the time the plate of cookies, and the couple's favourite brown teapot had been placed on the dining room table, scenic TV trays positioned in front of each person's chair, the tea poured and the cream and sugar cubes and the plate of cookies passed round, the latest prognosis had been covered.

Dr. Koffmann began. "Thank you, Mr. and Mrs. Ruhe, for letting us come see you on just two days notice. Thank you for letting us come see you at all. We realize this is strenuous for you, Mrs. Ruhe, but the work we have done so far would have been little more than a bother to you if we didn't continue as we discover things of interest in our research. Your case, is, as you know, a very interesting one, and your ability to withstand the radiation burns you received have been nothing short of astounding. Extraordinary, really. And just when we were running out of leads to our questions, our brilliant Linda, here, discovered something very interesting. And puzzling."

"We appreciate your coming all this way to see us," responded Jacob Ruhe. His wife gave him a quick glance that might have carried a signal to let the doctor speak, but he seemed not to notice.

"And the reason we're here is because we have discovered something that requires more work, more digging, and because we thought it easier at this point for us to travel than have you come our way again. We're hoping that we could find out more about you. We realize we've gone over a lot with you in our research already, but we might have missed something, and with the new information maybe we can discover what we need next."

"Has the cancer come back? Have you found something else?" queried the still nervous Jacob.

"Oh no, Mr. Ruhe," countered Dr. Koffmann quickly, "this is about needing more information for our research. There's no bad news in what we bring you today. At least I don't think so. As you may remember, we ran some DNA tests to try to find some correlations between people with similar DNA markings to yours, Mrs. Ruhe. To see if we could find someone else who had the same kind of resistance to radiation burns as you did. And that's where we came up with some interesting data. Can you tell me again where you were born and about your direct family background?"

"I was born in Gnadenheim, Barnaul Colony, in western Siberia, Russia," began Ruthie. "My parents were Anna and Cornelius Klassen. We left Russia and came to Canada in the 1920's when I was around twelve years old."

"What can you tell us about your parents' families?" asked Linda.

"I don't know much about my father's family, but my mother's parents were David and Elfrieda Ratzlaff. My parents lived with them. I don't remember them."

"And your mother, Anna? What do you know about her?"

"What do you mean, what do I know about her? She was born in the Ukraine, in a region called the Molotschna, moved a few times, married my father in a settlement called Neu Samara, and I was born not so long after they moved to Siberia. My mother had six children before she had me, and then another one after me, struggled with her health and with what everyone else struggled with in those difficult years in Russia and then came here to Canada. I don't know what else to say. She adjusted somewhat to life in Canada but died many years ago in British Columbia. But you seem to be asking me something more specific about her? What are you looking for?"

"Do you have, or did you ever see a birth certificate, or say, a baptism certificate, of your mother's?" continued Linda.

"No, I can't remember ever seeing a birth certificate. Or even a baptism certificate. I don't think we had such. Hmm." She paused to think. "Oh wait! I do remember an old postcard with a Bible verse she said her father had written on the back of and gave to her at her baptism. I remember her saying that she was baptized in Siberia in a stream, or a lake. She gave me that card on one of my last visits with her in British Columbia when she was getting very old. I think I still have it. But there was no baptism certificate. Just that postcard with the Bible verse written on it. I remember now, it was very important to her. She managed to hold on to that old postcard, it was a re-used Russian postcard, recycled we would say today, and she told me she brought it along to Canada stuck in the family Bible in a black wooden box when they came here. Here in Canada she kept it in a little cardboard box with her most precious possessions. Well, not many possessions. Who had much? But I remember a couple of pieces of jewelry, a pearl brooch, and a bent silver ring and that card that she wanted me to have before she died."

"Do you still have that postcard?" Dr. Kaufmann said. "Do you know or remember why it seemed so important to her?"

"It was important, I think, because it came from her father. It would have been all she had from him. But I should look for it. I'm sure I still have it here somewhere. I wouldn't have thrown it out." Ruthie Ruhe turned to her husband. "Jake, can you check my old jewelry case in the top draw of the tall dresser in our bedroom and see if that postcard is lying on the bottom under my old jewelry? Oh, that's funny, I even remember the verse now, it's 1 Peter 2:9, a well known Bible verse that tells the people how important they are. I know it from memory, it's: '*But you are a chosen people, a royal priesthood, a holy nation, a people belonging to God, that you may declare the praises of him who called you out of darkness into his wonderful light.'"*

Jacob had gone to the bedroom and now returned with a very tattered postcard in his hand that he handed to his wife. "Yes, this is it," she said, excitedly. "And here's what is so interesting in it. Grandpa added a word to the verse right at the beginning. Look. Let me read it. *'But you are (from) a chosen people, a royal priesthood, a holy nation, a people belonging to God, that you may declare the praises of him who called you out of darkness into his wonderful light.'"* I always wondered about that word *from* in brackets and I asked my mother but she didn't know either. I know we were taught to never add to Scripture, the Bible itself forbids it, but it looks like he really wanted to add some emphasis or something. Do you think?"

"I think it might be very significant, Mrs. Ruhe," said Dr. Koffmann. "May I see it?" Ruthie handed him the card. Glancing at the dark picture on the front of the card, the Doctor turned it over and narrowed his eyes to focus on the pointed printing. The letters were neat and unevenly coloured in shades of purple. He recognized from letters he had seen that his own grandfather had brought from Russia that the printing had been done with an indelible pencil, and the variation in the brightness and thickness of the lines was from different amounts of moisture on the pencil lead from having been dabbed on the writer's tongue. Dr. Koffmann looked up and asked, "Is this written in German, or in some other language?"

"German," smiled Ruthie. "Our people lived in Russia more than a hundred years but we were still speaking German. We lived in our own villages. Had our own schools. Only the men learned Russian for business," she laughed. "We are a stubborn people, changes don't come easily. We can't even change our minds most of the time," laughing again.

"Does anything get lost in the translation from the German to the English here?" Dr. Koffmann continued. "I do know German, but I was just wondering."

"I don't think so," said Jacob. He read the verse aloud in German pausing long enough to consider the addition to the text that Anna's father had made in the German. "What he did with the addition in German is the same as the word 'from' in English, and the meaning is the same. It seems he wanted mother, his daughter Anna, to know that not only was she a part of a chosen people in being baptized, but it seems he wanted to say that she was 'from' a chosen nation. Very curious! What was he thinking?"

"Do you think that your mother might have been adopted, Mrs. Ruhe?" asked Dr. Koffmann, glancing over at Linda.

"Adopted? Why would you ask that? Adopted? No! Not that I ever heard. I don't know how she could be. She was just another Mennonite girl like all the rest of them in her village. I think. She never said. We always thought that she had been born in the Mennonite village of Blumstein in Molotschna of the Ukraine. I think she would have told us she was adopted. Why? Lots of children lost their parents and were raised by others in Russia. The children even usually kept their family names. And everybody knew. It wasn't a secret. Why do you ask if my mother might have been adopted?"

"Well, the DNA test results, what we call your matrilineal DNA results, Mrs. Ruhe, those passed down from mothers to their children aren't consistent with the DNA markings usual in Mennonites. In fact, your matrilineal DNA markings are unique to Jewish people. Your mother, Anna Ratzlaff, we're sure, was Jewish."

Jacob and Ruthie looked at one another.

"Are you sure?" Jacob asked, an air of wonder in his voice.

"We're quite sure," answered the doctor.

Chapter 24
White Rock, Canada — 1997

The revelation, spoken twice, "You're my Dad! You're my Dad!" hung in the room, its power reverberating through the souls of two people. Elizabeth's because she had said it; Ben's because he had heard it. They sat in his office as if frozen. Someone called down the hallway that they were leaving, that the lights were out. "Just set the alarm when you leave," the voice added. While it was late in the afternoon when Elizabeth had arrived, the evening was now well advanced and they still sat.

It was Ben's turn to be quiet. Never in his entire life had he been so speechless. So incapable of finding any words. Ironically it was Ben who could not speak and Elizabeth finally moved to break the silence. She began very quietly. "You knew my mother as Liesbett Becker when you were in Germany. I saw her just a couple of months ago. Between, I think, the last time I was here, and the time before. I told her about you. About our visits. About how you know God. She asked a lot of questions. About you, your life, your family, what you did, your work. She said she had known what you would probably end up as, and laughed before she mumbled that you were more interested in God than in politics, that was clear. She asked what kind of person you were? Were you kind? Gentle? Teasing? I realized I didn't know much. She said she wanted me to get to know you. She was in the final stages of terminal cancer this last time I was there. I visited her in a palliative care facility. A month ago, I got the call that she died. She made me promise I wouldn't tell you about me and her, and you, until she was gone. She told me that you left Germany when you were twenty-one or so — that you had been friends, special friends, for a while — you both knew it couldn't last and that the two of you never talked again. She understood. You were just a boy, she said. She wasn't angry. She didn't blame you for going home. But she thought that you would want to know me. Do you want to know me?"

"I guess I don't even know myself," was all Ben could finally say. He was thinking a million thoughts, her poignant question just one of the jangling notions in his spinning mind. She stood up and was gone from the room before he realized her chair was empty. When he finally noticed, Ben jumped to his feet. Through his window he could see between the brilliant blossoms and branches of the rhododendron on the front lawn that her car was gone.

Ben had no phone number at which he could reach Elizabeth. He had no address for her. Nevertheless he searched for Elizabeth over the next few weeks and months, in every place he thought he might be able to find her. He made phone calls to people he thought might know her. He googled her name on the Internet. He tried to remember the names of the places where she worked, people he thought might know her. He visited playing fields where she might be playing soccer, she had talked about being a soccer player, but because he had never known from where she came and where she went, he had few options and fewer leads. He prayed for her and that he might find her. He wished he had one of her baseball hats that she usually wore to hang between the Jewish prayer shawl and the Palestinian *keffiyeh* on his coat rack. He really did want to know her. Could she know he really wanted to know her? How could he tell her? Was she staying away because he had been too stunned to say he wanted to know her that day?

Chapter 25
White Rock, Canada – 2002

Ben noticed the light blinking on his answering machine when he came into his place after work one Wednesday. He set to making dinner and forgot about the message waiting for his response until later in the evening. He pushed the button. "It's your Dad! We've got some very interesting news. Call us as soon as you get this message," came the familiar voice. Ben looked at the clock on the stove to see if it made sense to still call his father, two time zones ahead of him, and probably in bed by now. He picked up the phone anyway and pushed the numbers.

"What's up?" he asked as soon as he heard his father's voice. They talked often so there was little need for niceties or introductions. Their conversations were not necessarily deep nor profound most of the time, often just about the weather as a way to connect to hear one another's voices.

"I don't know if we told you that the doctor from Seattle who was doing research on how Mother survived her radiation was coming to talk to us again, but he and his assistant were here today. After some talk they dropped a real bombshell on us," his father said. "Yep, a real bombshell."

"What do you mean, a bombshell, Dad?" queried Ben. "It's usually the bomb that's the problem not the shell," trying to make a joke with his dad but a little annoyed as grown children often are at their aging parents' peculiar ways.

"Well you know that in all the research they did on Mother, one part was the DNA testing, eh? Well, they say they found out that your Grandmother Anna, Mom's mother, must be Jewish. That's what they found."

"Jewish! How could that be?"

"That's what we're wondering. Doesn't make sense. She was just a Mennonite like all the others, I thought. I know she was a little different, at times, everyone's different in some ways. You still remember her!"

"Yes, when she lived at the end in the nursing home. But she's Jewish! How could that be? Was she adopted? Were there Jewish people in the village Mom came from in Russia?"

"Lots of them, I've told you that. But they never lived in our villages, they just came and worked with us, or for us, and went back to their own villages, *shtetls* they called them, at night, or stayed in our haylofts if it was too late, or if they had more work in our villages that they wanted to finish the next day."

"But Grandma Anna. How could she be Jewish?"

"It's a mystery, but she was. 'No doubt about it,' says Dr. Koffmann. And his assistant, Linda, 'No doubt about it!' she said too. There's something about Mother's DNA that only Jews have and it comes from the mothers. So your grandmother Anna was Jewish. Boy oh boy, that's something! That means that your mom is Jewish, too, and if you're mom's Jewish, you're Jewish too. That's how they figure it. Who'd have guessed? And its funny with all your trips to Israel and all your studying Hebrew and on the kibbutz and everything. What do you think?"

Ben was silent. What did he think? He was reeling. He felt like he felt when Elizabeth had said "You're my Dad!" As if nothing in his being was solid anymore.

"You still there?" His father asked, shouting. "You still there? I think he hung up, Ruthie!" Ben heard him say to his mother. Ben imagined his dad's face turned away from the phone with his "confused by my children" look clouding it.

"No, I'm still here, Dad. My brain's running a million miles an hour, and I don't have any words. This is huge."

"Well, its not that huge," the elder man said.

"Yeah, it's that huge, Dad. It's enormous. It means the rest of the kids, and all our cousins on Mom's side, we're all genetically, racially, maybe even spiritually, religiously, if you will, Jewish. That's huge!"

"Well, I guess so," his dad always the leveler, sometimes the peacemaker, said. "So what? You all know who you are."

"No, Dad, we know who we are, but this really jangles our family mobile. At least mine."

"What do you mean, the 'family mobile'?"

"Oh, it's just an expression I use. Families are like kids' mobiles hanging over baby's beds. Either completely still in all their dysfunction, or bouncing up and down like crazy when something big happens. Like a death or a new baby. After that it tries to get back to the balance it had before. It's just education stuff, Dad. Counselling stuff I learned in school."

"Sounds weird."

"It is weird, but it's helpful. Sort of like broccoli or prunes, Dad, weird but helpful. Only this is about the way families work, not individuals. It doesn't matter."

"I thought I'd never say this, Ben, but sometimes I think you went to school too long. Learned too much," he chuckled.

"No, it wasn't too much, Dad. It just took me thirteen years of university to learn what you learned in six grades, that's all. It's not weird. It just is."

"Yeah, life is weird. Mom's wondering what being Jewish means right now. She says she wishes she would have known that when she worked as a maid in those Jewish homes in Winnipeg when she was young. 'She might have had a better deal,' I told her. I guess that wasn't nice. Anyway, I need to call your sisters. I called you first. You've always been more interested in this stuff. Call her sometimes, Ben, she doesn't feel very good very often. She cheers up a bit when you kids pay attention to her. Especially when she's sick. She's sleeping now."

"I'll call her tomorrow." Father and son both hung up. Ben stood by the phone, staring into space, trying to comprehend the news.

Chapter 26
Winnipeg-Cherry Creek — 2002

Ben Ruhe was scheduled to present a Family Systems workshop for a group of Mennonite clergy in Winnipeg. He usually tacked a few extra days onto the end of his schedule to visit his family in Cherry Creek whenever he was called to work in Winnipeg, and he did so again on this visit.

With his work finished he headed west along the familiar highway through open fields of various emerging crops, through prairie towns of hamburger drive-ins, implement dealers with acres of tractors, combines and sprayer rigs standing in straight lines, and three hours later, Ben was sitting with his ailing mother and his father who had become increasingly talkative as he grew older. The Jewish question never came up that first night. The next day Ben drove the fifteen kilometres or so to the tiny graveyard where his grandparents and a few other relatives were buried a mile north of a nearly abandoned prairie village. This little town had been the thriving centre of the community when he was young, with its three grain elevators, hardware and grocery stores, blacksmith shop, gas and service station, John Deere dealer, school and hockey and curling rink in winter, a half hour drive north and east of Cherry Creek. He remembered, too, that this village was where his father and mother were married in the pristine, little white church building that was still standing proudly and well kept in its little spot off the main street, a testimony to an important past now gone. As he got out of the car he noticed that high in the prairie sky an airplane traced a white line across the endless clear blue dome of the incredible heavens above. He walked through the open iron gate of the graveyard that was hedged in all around by late spring lilacs in their fine purple hues filling the air with their sweet, gentle perfume.

Ben was not surprised that there were only crosses on these gravesites and no Stars of David. But somehow he needed to check once he got there. He knew the graveyard well from the frequent visits he had made to this quiet and serene place with his father in his growing up years. He was not quite sure why he had come to the graveyard this morning, but suddenly his journey had become a "going back" as far as he physically and emotionally could, as he consciously began a reinvestigation of his identity. He could not yet know the depth of this journey but he was embarking on a complete re-assessment of who he was as a person, spiritually, religiously and emotionally in light of the information that he was ethnically not who he thought he was. He knew this journey would hold religious and cultural implications for him. He had known he was drifting into some identity confusion since his dad's call telling him that Grandma Anna was Jewish, of course, but he had never really let it come into the forefront of his thinking and feeling until he was home at the place of his own birth and upbringing, and re-entered the physical presence of his parents. Now at the graves of his grandparents even more feelings of wonder stirred within him. There was nothing physically in this graveyard, in the end, that would help him, he knew that would be the case, but he needed to start his journey somewhere and this seemed to be the place to start. Short of finding a way to go explore the places of the lost villages of the Ukraine and Siberia of his parents and grandparents, this graveyard was his ground zero.

As Ben knew he was alone in this graveyard far from anyone, he began to talk aloud, something his dad had often done when he thought he was alone. "Wow, my father is a Christian, a Mennonite, my grandmother and mother were Jewish, and I have a daughter I didn't know I had. Her grandfather was a Nazi. So, what am I? Who am I?"

Ben looked up to find the moving speck in the air drawing a thin white line across the sky and suddenly remembered the Jewish man in another airplane somewhere over the Atlantic years ago prophesying just such a moment as this for Ben, saying "You are the boy!"

He sat down and leaned against his grandmother's weathered headstone, the etching of her name barely distinguishable alongside her equally indistinguishable faded Siberian birthplace, Blumstein, the Ukraine, but, what he had never noticed before, there was no birth date. There was a birth date on his grandfather's headstone but not on his grandmother's. He would have to find out from his parents if they recalled any conversation about grandmother's birth date during her life or when she had passed away. Did they ever celebrate birthdays with her? Could they recall anything ever being said about the details of her birth, where she was born and when?

Ben's mind drifted to a combination of things Mennonite, things Jewish. He remembered the general agreement in the Jerusalem coffee shop years ago when he had declared that currently accepted Jewish orthodoxy in practice and the prevalently expressed beliefs of Christians were but a poor shadow of what they both were intended to be. He mused on his beliefs and tried to analyze the depth of his Christian convictions and devotion. He sat leaning against the old headstone for what must have been an hour before he finally got up and returned to his car. He drove back to Cherry Creek and his waiting parents.

DANNY UNRAU

A supper of homemade cabbage *borscht* and cottage-cheese *vereneke* with sweet cream sauce, reserved by his mother for visits from her children, all previously prepared and brought from their frozen state deep in the freezer and thawed and warmed by his dad on mother's clear instructions, was placed on the table. The three of them took their places at the table. Jacob Ruhe prayed a heartfelt thanksgiving prayer for their family, their son Ben and this present visit included, Mother's continued health, and for God's provision of the food before them. "In Jesus' name. Amen!" Ben grunted a matching "Amen!" In Jesus' name. Should he, could he, still pray that?

"So how are you doing, Mom, knowing that your mother was Jewish? Does it make any difference to anything?" asked Ben, after the first few mouthfuls of this much-loved meal of his heritage were enjoyed.

"I don't know. I haven't really felt well enough to think about anything very deeply, but it has caused me to wonder whether its our destiny to be Mennonites or Jews or anything else when we're born, and can the path be changed?" she smiled.

"Do you remember any indication, any conversation when you were young that Grandma might be Jewish?"

"Nothing!"

"Did your family ever talk about Jews, Mom? And were there any Jewish people around your village?"

"Oh, there were Jewish people around," Jacob chimed in. "We had a tailor who would stay with us and who was a friend of your Grandfather's, but that was a different village from Mother's. And we prayed on Friday nights like the Jews prayed until the troubles started. We were very aware in our villages of the Jews and their ways. We Mennonites had much in common with the Jews."

"What trouble?" Ben turned toward his Dad.

"With the armed bands coming around. Taking things, our horses, stealing food. Even bothering the girls and the women. But we Mennonites didn't want to fight, and I remember that they were far worse with the Jews than they were with us Mennonites. And what they did with us was bad enough. I remember that's when the village families decided to not circumcise their sons anymore."

"Not circumcise? Why was that?

"So that the Mennonite boys couldn't ever be mistaken for Jewish boys. Our leaders saw that might be a problem down the road as things were getting worse. So our doctors stopped the cutting. Sometimes the roving gangs made the boys show whether they were 'Jew boys' or not. And like I said, the special Friday dinners that we had learned from the tailor stopped, too. I don't know about Mother's village. Do you remember?" he turned toward Ruthie but did not wait for an answer. "Their village wasn't that far from ours. I remember my dad worried that he might hurt the tailor who sewed all the clothes for the people in our village at our place that we didn't want to be mistaken for Jews, or didn't want to help them when they were in trouble. But the church leaders said we had to defend ourselves somehow. I was too young to be at the men's meetings there were about what should be done, but Grandpa told me some of the things and I heard the talk from the older boys."

"Is that why I wasn't circumcised as a newborn baby boy in Cherry Creek? So that no one would mistake me for a Jew?" Ben asked. His parents glanced at one another.

"Sometimes we know the rules, but no one can remember why we made the rule in the first place. And rules we've known for a long time are not easy to unmake," his father said.

"So you remember that there were many Jewish villages in the area? And you remember that the Mennonites tried not to associate too closely with them?"

"Yes, there were a number of Jewish villages outside of our settlement and it's true we never really went to any of them. They always came our way and some of our Mennonites weren't very friendly, but your grandfathers, I remember, on both sides, they had good relationships with the Jewish men who came to our villages. That's probably where you got your good attitude toward Jews. Without knowing it, you inherited it. The good and bad attitudes of family pass down. Even the Bible says that." The conversation trailed off, evolved into a silence of thinking and more wondering.

"Oh by the way, Ben, I just remembered your grandmother Anna, once when we were there visiting her in the nursing home before she died, she talked about getting to know two Jewish women who lived there. I remember she had said it was funny how much she liked them, 'more than the Mennonites.' I even remember she said she felt like she had more in common with them and she had laughed. She was funny. Interesting, eh?"

With the supper dishes cleared up, Mother reported who were the latest ill-health victims in the neighbourhood and the church, who it was that was sick now and who had had surgery. Ben's dad just kept talking about everything that came to mind. As he aged the subjects were increasingly left out of his sentences and Ben had to force himself to listen carefully so he would know who or what his father was talking about. He was tired and his mind was drifting elsewhere.

After his parents had gone to bed, Ben phoned his travel agent in Vancouver. "Can you book me a flight to Tel Aviv out of Winnipeg," he asked, "with a return to Vancouver in a couple of weeks?" He next called his church board chair, and left a message that he was taking three additional weeks away. He knew that his strange behaviour and last minute changes would cause some raised eyebrows in his congregation, but this trip was something he had to do.

Chapter 27
Jerusalem – Vancouver – Winnipeg – 2002

Ben found a room in the Jewish quarter of the Old City of Jerusalem as quickly as he could after the taxi driver dropped him off at the corner of the wall just west of Zion Gate. He had never stayed in the Jewish Quarter in any of his previous visits to the Holy City, but it felt necessary this time. The sun was sinking low in the sky so without unpacking his few belongings Ben left his room and snaked his way through the familiar narrow limestone streets and alleyways down to the Western (Wailing) Wall. Jews of every conceivable tradition met him coming up into the city as he descended the stairs toward the large courtyard of the Wall. Ben wondered whether he would feel a new kinship with the Jewish people as he returned to this city in which he had always felt a connection, now intensely mindful that his own heritage was Jewish. Surprisingly, he felt nothing new. Not even excitement. Just determination. But he was curious. Ben became conscious that he had emotionally stepped outside of himself, as if he had removed his emotions from his body and was looking in on himself. He realized that what he had come to Jerusalem for was about needing conversation regarding identity, not checking his emotions and feelings. He knew he would not be able to do that reflectively though; he needed to think aloud, through back and forth exploratory conversations with others.

Ben formed a strategy for such conversations. For his own discovery. He set himself mentally for a week of verbal exchanges that could trigger introspection and profound questioning, deep soul searching and self-discovery.

He did not stay long at the Wall and surprisingly entered into no conversations. It was as if he was simply getting his bearings. He trudged back to his lodgings and went to bed.

Jet-lagged, Ben slept late the next morning. His sleep had been light and disturbed by what felt like hours of wakefulness caused by an over-active mind. He had been aware of the silence of the sleeping city, a city without cars, then aware of heels on cobblestone streets, dawn-breaking street sweepers, early morning delivery men, window casements being opened, carpets being beat, children heading for *shul*, and various vendors shouting out their wares and services. He finally emerged from his room close to noon and with his laptop computer bag strap hiked up high on his shoulder, headed out of the Old City. Once through Zion Gate he turned west and south before passing the Jewish Yeshiva and the Armenian Seminary, and then the Jerusalem University College, before dropping down into the Hinnom Valley, where in biblical days the garbage was constantly burning, giving the ancient prophets, priests and rabbis a visual picture of what hell might be like. Up the other side of the valley, Ben hurried past the Scottish Hospice and gained the busy street known as Emek Refaim along the shallow valley, which many thousands of years earlier was known to the biblical King David.

This morning Ben was hoping he might be able to find a seat and the atmosphere conducive in the Emek Refaim *Aroma* Coffee Bar to recreate conversations like the one he had had there some years before with nearly a restaurant full of people discussing clashing Christian and Jewish issues and perceptions. With the vague hope that the young man named Doron, who had been key in that earlier conversation might again be in the *Aroma*, Ben studied the faces drinking coffee and enjoying the usual Israeli breakfast before he even looked for a seat for himself. There was, however, no space to be found. The room was full, overly full, and a small line-up of hopefuls waited outside the door. Not that waiting followed any kind of order or decorum in this country. Space that came clear was always gained by the fleetest of foot and those who were the most creative in their movement across a room, not those who had waited the longest. As Ben waited for a place to come free, he thought of another place where a helpful conversation might take place. He stepped out of the coffee bar line-up and turned west on Rachel Immaneu Street and angling slightly in a northwest direction walked through the residential German Quarter with its politically controversial Christian Embassy and striking Arab homes hemmed-in by cascading, brilliantly enflamed bougainvillea trees. Up the hill in the direction of the Jerusalem Theatre, Ben hurried as if he had to complete something most important as soon as was possible. Had he continued up and over the hill in the direction he was taking, he would have soon dropped down into the valley next to St. George's *Monastery of the Cross* just below the Knesset, but at the top of the rise he turned left into Hapalmach Street. He had come this way remembering the outdoor coffee and sweets restaurant squeezed between a grocery store and a bank where a group of political journalists sat and drank coffee, smoked, shouted and shared stories every day of the week but the Sabbath.

Ben had never sat and talked with these men; he had been too intimidated by their swagger and typically Israeli opinionated approach to seemingly everything. Israeli journalists, as he had observed their behaviour the many times he had passed this place in earlier times, reminded him of the sportswriters he had come to know in Canada, people who had an attitude of knowing everything about everything and completely unafraid to tell anyone their "truth." But the mission he was on today trumped his insecurity around these journalists about whom he personally knew nothing. He ordered a cappuccino and a semi-sweet cinnamon pastry from the surly outdoor waiter and sat down at a table next to the raucous men who, exactly as he remembered, were exchanging stories and opinions in loud voices and with dramatic gestures.

Ben remained unnoticed, feeling meek beside these characters, until his coffee cup was half empty and his cinnamon dessert was finished. Finally he caught the eye of a fifty-something raconteur with his hat pushed back on his head and he ventured, "Excuse me, I'm a Mennonite farm boy from Canada, may I ask you a question?" Whether it was his soft gentleness over against the journalist's inherent energy, or the words Mennonite or Canada, the men all stopped their shouting in mid-sentence and turned toward Ben.

"Mennonite?" said the man he had addressed. "Aren't they a Christian sect that came out of Russia late in the 1800s and early in the 1900s and went to places like Mexico, and South and North America?"

"Yes?" said Ben, astonished at his quick and fortuitous entry into the group conversation. "That's true, but I have a question of you gentlemen."

Some of the journalists rolled their eyes at being called gentlemen signalling their concurrence that the use of the term was a typically North American kind of flattery that Israelis have no tolerance of — but it seemed they found Ben too unique in the middle of their den to dismiss him just yet. "I've been in Israel on a number of occasions, volunteered on a kibbutz, been in every corner of this country, and earned a Master's degree in Judaism on Mt. Zion. I once rented a flat just around the corner from here on Tchernikovsky Street. I love this place, but no one has ever been able to answer for me why in the whole Israeli attempt to convince the world that it deserves to be here where it is, against all the Arab resistance, after the known existence of the First Jewish Commonwealth of the first Temple era, and the second Jewish Commonwealth under the Maccabeans until the Roman destruction, why the leaders of the modern state of Israel after 1948 haven't loudly and internationally referred to modern Israel as the Third Jewish Commonwealth? It would have given the whole world a sense of Israel's continuity. As it is, you're seen as a bunch of interlopers and upstarts, Zionist fanatics and religious zealots, a country which came out of nowhere and occupied and threw out the people who had been here forever!"

For a brief second that felt like longer, Ben's band of journalists sat still and unspeaking. Never short of opinions, it was as if the normally unruly crowd of Knesset political watchers needed a second to collect their thoughts.

"Because calling it the Third Jewish Commonwealth would have suggested a kind of racism in its being a Jewish nation," came the first answer "and our early leaders didn't want to give ground to such a suggestion."

"Racism is a concept that wasn't even thought of in 1948," came a dissenting voice, but then another turned the tide of the conversation, and true to form an argument broke out.

"What's your interest? What makes a Mennonite farm boy from Canada interested in the Third Jewish Commonwealth? I think your question is coming from a larger issue for you than the politics of world opinion. Am I right?" The questioner's words rattled like a machine gun attack and Ben fought down the feeling of being a little boy challenged by big boys and wanting to run from the danger and intensity.

"I thought it might be a good question to begin a conversation with men of your knowledge and experience," Ben responded. "And I think you people at these tables might be the best of anyone I know to answer that question. But you're right, I might have a larger agenda." He grinned.

"Well you've started something here," laughed the questioner at one of the tables. "So what's your story, boy?" Ben wondered how many decades it had been since anyone had called him a boy, and he wondered whether at this moment if it was just a coincidence or something to do with destiny.

A tall, thin twenty-something Hasidic man in characteristic black clothes, white shirt, large brimmed fedora and dangling side-curls stopped at one of the tables to ask one of the journalists for a light of his cigarette as a young orthodox woman looking stressed rolled her stroller with toddler twins up to Ben's table and began to ask a question in Hebrew. Ben told her in Hebrew that he didn't speak the language. Switching to English in a New York accent she said, "I have to make a phone call in the deli, please watch my twins. Make sure they don't get separated or converted while I'm gone!" She must have heard some of the conversation between Ben and the coffee drinkers around the tables and somehow trusted him more than his rambunctious companions, although there is an assumption in Israel that people, even strangers, look after one another when there is a need. So the request to mind her children was not that unusual.

"See those twins?" said one of the journalists. "They'll not live the same lives. Twins never do. Even you have lived at least two lives." He smiled at Ben. "But you still haven't answered what makes you so interested in things Jewish that you keep coming back."

A cell phone rang in someone's pocket and every one of the combatants at the tables reached for his phone. The mother of the twins came back to collect her children and hurried off without a word. Suddenly Ben felt not ready, not quite safe, nor even quite in the right setting to explore the deep questions wanting exploring or asking. A black police car its blue lights flashing sped by on Hapalmach within a metre of the sidewalk tables. The moment Ben had been wanting with these men was clearly lost. He saw the drop in their interest and intensity and took the pause to grab his bag. He stood up and followed in the direction of the young mother and her twins. The journalists accepted his appearance and even quicker departure as one of the norms of life on the street of western Jerusalem. When he gained Tchernikovsky, the street on which he had once rented a flat, Ben did not turn left to walk past it. Instead he turned toward the city centre and in the direction of the Old City itself. Another idea had come into his head. Now it seemed place and symbol were more important than conversation, and faith more important than politics. His adrenaline was up; his spirit was spinning.

Ben's brisk walk raised beads of sweat on his forehead as he gained the height of the city, crossed King George Street and headed down toward the Jaffa Gate. With barely a glance he passed the Paris-like shops of the Mamila Shopping Centre before striding up the steps and into the completely contrasting hubbub just inside the ancient Jaffa Gate with its quarrelling taxi-drivers, young boys selling their sesame seed *bagelas*, stalking business owners and wide-eyed tourists and pilgrims.

Ben entered the narrow David Street and descended down between the shops of the Arab *souk* to HaNotsrim, the first street to the left, and followed it past the German Lutheran Church and to the courtyard outside the door of the Church of the Holy Sepulchre. There was no more significant symbol of Christianity for Ben than this site, no matter how much a Protestant, never mind a Mennonite might be confused by the icons and the incense, to say nothing of the potential violence amongst the monks from any one of the seven major Christian traditions sharing this site, all demanding their right to protect Jesus' most sacred memory. None of these issues bothered Ben this morning. He was searching for himself in the midst of the Christian symbolism this day and no monks, shopkeepers, or pilgrims of any stripe would be a distraction.

He even knew where he would go next. He headed for the centrepiece of the Holy Sepulchre, the Rotunda or the Aedicule as it was also known, having paused briefly inside the wide doors of the Church at the remembered site of Golgotha, the Rock of Calvary, and the Stone of Anointing right at the entrance, still and almost always wet from the tears of pilgrim women in black dresses who wept over the stone purported to be where Jesus' body was prepared for burial so long ago. Ben was moved by their emotion. He marveled at their expressed connection to the object of their devotion.

The Church of the Holy Sepulchre had since his very first visit amazed Ben. It always filled him with mixed revulsion and awe. What being in this place had to do with his faith and his spiritual connection to Jesus he never quite understood, and he stopped and waited for some emotion connecting him to the mystical Christ. He pushed past some elderly nuns about to enter the Rotunda of Jesus' tomb, and with uncharacteristic *chutzpah* he knelt on the marble floor in the small first room of the Aedicule. Among the hanging incense burners and garish décor of what was medieval Christendom, Ben sought the spirit of Christ deep in his heart. The Greek or Catholic Orthodox nuns gathering around him and jostling for position, he never noticed. Ben could not remember how long he knelt, not knowing whether he was summoning or waiting for a flame or a whisper from the spirit of Jesus.

It must have been near four o'clock when Ben pulled his Tilley hat, until now crunched into a ball in his hand, onto his head and walking east from the Church of the Holy Sepulchre, turned left into the narrow, noisy Arab market street again and headed for the Damascus Gate. His next destination was the Garden Tomb outside the city wall, across and down the street from Sultan Suileman Street. He stepped past village Arab women in black dresses with red embroidered trim and bibs carrying huge bundles of what looked like grape and mint leaves on their heads, and Muslim men talking in bunches fingering unconsciously and habitually through their prayer beads.

He turned up into the little alley that took him to the door of the serene Garden Tomb. Once inside a pleasant man with an English accent and a pale complexion wanted to engage Ben in conversation about his specific interest in the tomb. Ben was not interested in polite and light conversation this day and drew himself away from his host as quickly as he could without appearing rude. He knew the Garden well. He angled toward the small recessed courtyard fronting the small tomb carved into the limestone rock face below a gentle hill. This was believed by some to be that of the biblical Joseph of Arimathea into which the body of Jesus had been laid. This tomb was simply empty and appealed to western Protestants' spiritual sensitivities more than did the ornately decorated Holy Sepulchre's Aedicule with its incense burners and other symbols of high church.

Ben bent over and entered the tomb. It was the size of a small bedroom. He leaned against the wall and stared at the space carved out of the floor for placing a dead body. Ben breathed deeply, not expecting a visitation. But he would have welcomed one. A deep peace descended on his body and quieted his spirit. With no else present in the tomb, Ben sat down on the floor and leaned against the wall of what was a tiny anteroom to the burial site itself. He pulled his knees up and rested his chin on his arms. He let his mind wander and wonder. A tear formed in the corner of his eye and he wondered if he might just be a little like the Greek Orthodox women crying at the Table of Anointing in the Church of the Holy Sepulchre after all. He was not sure, why, though, he was crying. Jesus' dying, all human death, was part of it to be sure, but this emotion was more. Would the death of Jesus have to cease to be meaningful to him if he were Jewish? His spiritual identity was here, he thought. It was unmistakably tied to Jesus, it was too strong. It could not be denied. His heart was at home here, and yet, some unsettledness still stirred within him. "Is there more?" he wondered, "or is this as good as it gets? Is this feeling in this quiet tomb of Jesus the essence of being spiritual for me?"

Ben sat undisturbed for another forty-five minutes before a pair of Scandinavian pilgrims stuck their heads into the tomb, surprised and a little embarrassed that they had disturbed Ben in his deep reverie. Startled, Ben welcomed the two into the tiny sacred space with an inviting wave and a smile and ducked out of the tomb. He nodded to the Englishman still standing guard at the garden gate and stepped from the peace of the Garden Tomb into the hubbub of Arab East Jerusalem. Reaching the Damascus Gate, Ben turned right along the outside of the ancient wall of the city and walked toward Joffa Road. When he reached Joffa road he turned right again planning to follow it until it crossed King George Street, but at Zion Square he turned into Ben Yehuda Street. No car traffic was allowed here and its jewelry stores, banks, *kippah* shops, *falafel* stands and businesses of a great variety were busy along the walking mall.

Ben walked up the gentle lift of Ben Yehuda. He heard a street musician playing Eric Clapton's "Father's Eyes" on an electric guitar on the street corner and he sat down on the edge of a large planter flowing over with bright flowers of many colours to take in the wide panorama of the busy street, and listen to and watch the musician at the same time. He could see a small group of Orthodox Jewish men with a table of ready *phylacteries* stopping any Jewish men they could to urge them to pray for the sake of spreading Jewish faithfulness and righteousness in the land of Israel. Ben had approached these evangelistic Jewish zealots before, but when he mentioned he was Christian they had politely told him his job was to help Jews be good Jews, that he did not need to pray.

As Ben listened to the music wondering at its spiritual implications, all the while still keeping an eye on the dynamic busyness around him, someone tapped him on the shoulder. A young woman who by her conservative dress and head covering could easily pass for an Orthodox Jewish woman asked him if she could give him something. "Sure!" he said. She handed him a handbill. It had its message printed in English on one side and Hebrew on the other. "You are invited," it read, "to a Jewish-Christian meeting at the Narkis Street Church to pray for the peace of Jerusalem this Thursday evening at 8:00 p.m." Ben smiled at the young woman as she moved on, offering her notice to others. Since he had just been invited to Christian prayer he got up and approached the young men trying so hard and enthusiastically to get passersby to don their *teffillin* and say the traditional Jewish prayers. "My grandmother was Jewish," he told them. "May I pray?"

"Stretch out your left arm," said a smiling, sparsely bearded young man with an open necked white shirt and a wide-rimmed black hat pushed back on his head as he picked up one of the phylacteries from the table.

The next morning Ben flagged down a *sherut* to the Ben Gurion airport, negotiated his open airline ticket to return to Vancouver with a largely disinterested Israeli Air Canada agent, and was back in his home before he could adjust to whatever new realities now lived in his realized identity. He spent a few days in the spectacular beauty of another complicated city that pushed up between ocean and mountain, clearing up unfinished and necessary business, and then went to the airport to board a plane back to Winnipeg. He felt he needed to begin this new journey where he had begun. In his carry–on bag he carried a few daily essentials and one change of clothes. On top of his clothes he had placed a carefully wrapped linen Jewish prayer shawl and his specially selected Russian-made *yarmulke* for the Saturday he would spend in a synagogue he would find in that city, and beside it, a leather bound New Testament for his Sunday visit to a Mennonite church. He felt free and whole, complete and alive.

At the airline gate Ben entered into a stimulating conversation with a pair of unusually relaxed airline employees about how multicultural and faith diverse their city and Canada had become. When it was time to board, Ben inadvertently left his carry-on bag at the counter. He did not miss it, however, until one of the Air Canada employees he had spoken to earlier at the check-in came down the aisle toward him carrying his bag, "I think this is yours, Mr. Ruhe. I'm sorry we had to open it to find out whose it was, and to make sure it was safe to bring it aboard. We found your name on a Jewish prayer book and on a New Testament. For security reasons, I need to ask, 'Did you pack the contents of this bag? Are you the person who owns this carry-on and its contents?"

Ben smiled, "I am! I am!"

Glossary

"Arbeit Macht Frei"
— "Work Will Set You Free" Nazi slogan of WW 2 concentration camps. (German)

Baader-Meinhof Gruppe
— radical, left-wing, revolutionary group active in Germany in the 1970's & 80's

bagelas
— oval-shaped sesame seed bread sold from open carts by Arab vendors in the streets of old Jerusalem

borscht
— Ukrainian/Mennonite cabbage soup

burdei
— half-dugout log & sod shelter of the Ukraine

Chai
— Life; root of the Hebrew celebratory term "La Chaim — to life!" (Hebrew)

chnibbler
— village trained chiropractor/masseuse (Low German)

chutzpah
— audacity, nerve, spunk (Yiddish)

davening
— prayer (Yiddish)

"Deutschland, Deutschland Über Alles"
— "The Song of Germany" used on and off as the national anthem of Germany since 1922.

dhimi
— attitude of submission (Arabic)

Die Russa
— The Russians (German)

Erez Yisrael
— The land of Israel (Hebrew)

falafel
— street food of the Middle-East consisting of a pita pocket filled with deep-dried chick pea balls, salad & sauces.

faspa
— light meal zwieback, pickles, cheese, cold cuts and *platz* (sweet crumbly dessert) commonly served on Sunday evenings in Mennonite homes

Fussballs
— footballs

Galill
—the vicinity of the Sea of Galilee

Gottesdienst
— worship service (German)

grüben smaltz
— cracklings, crispy drippings & remnants of deep fried pork ribs

"Grüss Gott"
> — a south German greeting that literally means, "Greet God"

HaShem
> — "The Name" a more casual term for referring to God used to avoid using one of the more direct names for God (Hebrew)

"Herr Gott Sacrament"
> — a religious expletive (German)

Jeshuah
> — Jesus (Hebrew)

keffiyeh
> — traditional Arab male head dress fashioned from a square scarf

Kanadier
> — Canadian (German)

Khirgiz
> — people of the Khirgiz, a republic of the former Soviet Union

kibbutzim
> — plural for kibbutz, the communal farms credited with early social, economic and political development in modern Israel

kibbutzniks
> — kibbutz members.

kippah/yarmulke
> — skullcap worn by religious Jewish males

kosher
— Jewish food regulations

Kulaks
— derisive term for land owner in revolutionary Russia

kvas
— non-alcoholic Russian drink made from rye bread, sometimes flavoured with herbs & fruit

lebensraum
— living room (German)

leba wurst
— liver sausage (German)

"Mach schnell"
— "Hurry up!" (German)

melamed
— teacher/scholar; usually one who had just enough learning to teach little boys how to pray, read and memorize the Bible (Hebrew)

mensch
— person of character/substance/notice

mezuzah
— small box attached to observant Jewish door post containing biblical texts

minyan
— quorum required for Jews to conduct a religious service

"one hand on their swords"
— (Nehemiah 4:16 — The Bible) reference to the returned exiles re-building the wall of Jerusalem with one hand

and holding a weapon in the other to protect themselves against their opponents

Operation Nachshon
— Jewish military operation in 1948 to open the road from Tel Aviv to Jerusalem

Pale of Settlement
— area in western Russia to which Jews were restricted by the Russian Tsars from 1791 to 1917

perishky
— Mennonite fruit or meat-filled pastry

phylacteries
— English term for teffilin (see below)

portzelky
—deep-fried "New Year's Fritters"

Prediger
— minister/pastor/preacher (German)

Rebbe
— rabbi (Yiddish)

rebspair
— pork ribs (Low German)

roubles
— Russian currency

sauber frauen
— cleaning women (German)

Scheisskommando
— excrement/waste removal team (German)

schlepping
   — carry, drag, move (Yiddish)

Schwäbs
   — persons of Swabia, a state in south-western Germany

Shabbas
   — Sabbath (Yiddish)

sherut
   — a set route taxi service

shtetl
   — Jewish village (Yiddish)

Shukran
   — "Thank you!" (Arabic)

shul
   — school (Yiddish)

Sicarri
   — political zealots (sometimes violent) during the Second Temple Period in Jerusalem

souk
   — outdoor market (Arabic)

Sozialistischer Deutscher Studentenbund
   — Socialist German Student Union

Staatsoper
   — State Opera House

stadia
   — an ancient unit of measurement of 185 metres

sukkah
— a booth built to celebrate the Jewish festival of
Booths (Sukkoth)

steppe
— Siberian plain

tefillin
— phylacteries — two black boxes containing biblical
texts that religious Jewish men attach to their foreheads
and forearms in prayer-time

Unter den Linden Strasse
— main street in East Berlin

vereneke
— Mennonite version of perogies (dumplings filled with
cottage cheese or fruit

verst
— obsolete Russian unit of length of approximately
1.07 kilometres.

vopos
— East German border guards stationed along the
Berlin Wall

yarmulke/kippah
— skullcap worn by religious Jewish males

zwieback
— double-decker buns traditionally served at faspa and
Mennonite festive events